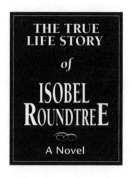

THE TRUE
LIFE STORY

of

ISOBEL
ROUNDTREE

A Novel

THE TRUE
LIFE STORY

of

ISOBEL
ROUNDTREE

A Novel

KATHLEEN WALLACE KING

AUGUST HOUSE PUBLISHERS, INC.
LITTLE ROCK

Published 1993 by August House, Inc.,
P.O. Box 3223, Little Rock, Arkansas 72203, 501-372-5450.

Printed in the United States of America

10 9 8 7 6 5 4 3 2

LIBRARY OF CONGRESS CATALOGING-IN-PUBLICATION DATA
King, Kathleen Wallace, 1959-
The true life story of Isobel Roundtree:
a novel / by Kathleen Wallace King.
p.   cm.
ISBN 0-87483-263-2 : $19.00
1. Family—Indiana—Fiction.
2. Girls—Indiana—Fiction. I. Title.
PS3561.I4798T78   1993
813'.54—dc20 93-22724

Executive editor: Liz Parkhurst
Assistant editors: Nancy King, Sue T. Williams
Design director: Ted Parkhurst
Cover design: Byron Taylor
Typography: Heritage Publishing Co.

Lyrics from "Stormy Monday" are used by permission.
Copyright© 1963 Gregmark Music, Inc. (renewed).
All rights reserved.

This book is printed on archival-quality paper that meets the
guidelines for performance and durability of the Committee on
Production Guidelines for Book Longevity of the
Council on Library Resources.

AUGUST HOUSE, INC.   PUBLISHERS   LITTLE ROCK

F
KIN

To Larkin for being.
To Kurt for believing.

"Man that is born of a woman is of few days, and full of trouble."

—JOB 14:1

"Turn off that damn TV and go read a book."
—WARREN COLVIN KING

one

Here it is

Let's get this clear before we go anywhere. I'll be telling this story. This is my life story up to now and it isn't always pretty. Emma's always after me saying, "Why don't you write about pretty things?" I can't say that life's always pretty. I knew that anyway but now I know it double.

I'm writing this out of pure memory. That whole year that passed? I memorized it. I memorized it the way you do when you have a moment you always want to remember—you know—you take a picture. Say you're feeling especially happy, something good happened, like someone says you're smart as a whip, or you smell good, or even something bad happens, like you see a dog get killed—or worse—you take a picture, click, in your head and then you've always got it with you. You can take out that picture anywhere and examine it up close, but what's even better than a paper picture is that you get those smells— odors that cling to the memory *and* you get the feel. Feel meaning those things that plant themselves into your brain and keep that memory separate from others. The feel of your heart beating—thump, thump, thump, thump—the feel of touch—you touching, someone touching you—the feel in your gut at the moment that thing happened, whether it eats your stomach up to remember or makes it floaty, filled with butterfly wings. The feel of the world at that moment because for you, the world stopped while you took the picture.

I write this starting at the moment that the pictures start to feel especially important. My life story really begins in November 1963, even though I was alive for eleven years before that time and I will be including some things from then. But really, up to then it was just the buildup. But that's what I've come to know. Its all just a buildup. And you keep building and building without ever getting to the top. Who knows where the very tiptop is? Or what's there? Climbing and building we go and its like we're some kind of underground animals without eyes, sniffing for fresh air, thinking there's light at the top even though we can't see anything but darkest underground night. We just keep climbing and each step is a memory.

two

On her way to the devil

The night before John F. Kennedy got shot, my momma ran off again. I thought this time she was surely gonna die.

We'd all been down in the living room watching Red Skelton. I was sitting on the rug that my great grandma had braided in the convent and my momma kept flipping through a *Life* magazine without even looking at it. I sneaked a look over at my dad and he was watching her too.

"Look at that," said my dad when Red Skelton did his slowmotion man. "That something, honey?" My momma didn't look up.

"Hey, yeah," I said to my dad, "but I like him best when he does that sad old bum." It took me awhile but I'd finally figured out that the man that did the show was named Red Skelton and there never was a real red skeleton.

My momma didn't hear either one of us, or else she was pretending not to. What she did do was get up out of her chair and stretch, arms out front and then over her head. She reached back, tore out the rubber band and shook down that red fire hair.

"Doesn't that hurt, Momma?" I asked. She had hair that could break your heart, reaching down the way it did to the middle of her back, arranging itself naturally in soft, shiny waves. My hair is the color of tree bark, or maybe I could describe it better by saying its more like the color of cow pies that have dried up in the sun. I'm not being cute—I have hair that's no real color at all.

"Don't feel it," said my momma. She started moving around the living room, eating up space, looking out a window, tapping the arm of a chair. I looked back to the television, brand new two months ago, a big console set with doors that closed over the picture tube. A car commercial had come on.

"Where you going, honey?" asked my dad as she left the living room. "Don't bother yourself with those dishes." He knew she wasn't going anywhere near the kitchen, though. We gave each other that look, the look that traded each other's thoughts. From down the hallway my momma's voice came to us, cold and high. "I need a drink."

My dad wouldn't look at me when I did a shadow puppet on the shade of the standing lamp. "Look, daddy, it's a flying horse." I flapped my fingers to get the wings to fly.

Red Skelton came back on. From the bedroom my dad and me heard the radio playing "Breathless." Shake, rattle, and roll was my momma and we both knew it. Her restlessness crept down the hallway and wrapped around our throats. A few minutes later she came back in the living room dressed to go out—full shiny purple dress with a wide belt that sparkled with diamonds and rubies at her waist.

I ran to her as she picked the car keys up off the end table by the sofa. My dad stared at the TV.

I stood there in front of her. "Look, Momma," I said, "I need braces bad." I pulled my mouth wide open so she could see my jaggedy teeth.

She wouldn't look. She moved around the living room picking up first a newspaper, then a fat stuffed pillow with embroidered apples. "Either of you seen my pocketbook?" Sharp-voiced, mean-edged.

"My teeth are fangs!" I went up right in front of her. I blocked her way out of the room.

"Get away from me," she said.

"If you go, don't come back," said my dad.

I grabbed my momma's hand, the one with the little diamond heart ring, and I bit her, hard, between her thumb and first finger. My teeth left little craters that filled in red with blood. Well, that stopped her—she stood there staring at her hand.

My dad blasted out of his recliner and slapped me silly. I took off spinning and hit the wall. I skidded down the wall to the floor and stayed there, pretending to be unconscious, but neither one of them looked so I just sat there by the peeling wallpaper.

My momma was leaving. I heard the screen door slam. "You heard me," said my dad. "You heard me," he screamed. I could hear her clip, clip, clipping in her dainty princess high heels across the front porch. I'd been hiding in my hair, but now I brushed it back and saw my dad standing in the center of the living room. He was looking at the screen door trying to bring my momma back with the force of his stare.

Some Indians were paddling a canoe on the TV. They brushed their teeth with Pepsodent. I touched my slap and knew it'd leave a big red mark on my face.

Now it was my dad and me and this time I felt sure she'd stay gone. My mother, her name's Clematis, left us lots of times before, but she always made a big show of it—packing up her bags, slamming closet doors, taking her little china knickknacks off the mantle and usually breaking at least one while we, my dad and me, just sat in the recliners and watched TV. We'd pretend we didn't notice that she was tearing our world apart. We'd sit there, the blue and white light streaming out to us from the TV set, all wrapped up in a blanket of pictures and sound. My dad, the Prince, would talk to me very clear and distinct over that sound, saying things that didn't mean anything but were like a code—"Miss Kitty is looking fatter this week." And I'd say, "I think she looks fat, too."

What we meant was we both understood that we couldn't show Clematis anything, no anger and definitely no tears. That'd just make her meaner, just make her nastier. If she'd been drinking more than normal she'd stand in front of the TV before she left, blocking our view, trying to rile us up. But we stuck together and she couldn't get anything out of us. She'd load up the Chevy with her knickknacks and suitcase and drive who knows where or just fall asleep out there in the car. When she actually left she wasn't ever gone more than one week.

But this time she didn't take anything—not even the china bulldog. The china bulldog was all chipped and cracked because she usually took him first thing of all—she'd just toss him in a sack. No matter how beat up that china bulldog got she never threw it out—she said it reminded her of somebody. This time she wasn't really even drunk. This time she got dressed up like she was really going somewhere. She hadn't tried to fight, she hadn't called my dad a bum, she hadn't even told me that I couldn't possibly be her own daughter. She hadn't even said, "I hate this goddamned hole and *all you pigs* in it!"

When I heard the car screech out, burning up the tires, I was sure she was going to die. Slam into a ditch, bang into a telephone pole—that car told how crazy she was, it told me she just didn't care.

My dad wouldn't look at me. I heard him going down the hallway, then I heard the bedroom door close. I got myself up off the floor, feeling the wall across my backbone. I went up to my bedroom and hid under the covers from all the shadows that crept across my nighttime walls. I have always been afraid of ghosts, but that night I was more afraid of human beings. Ghosts, at least, seemed pretty predictable—

they'd haunt you, you'd get scared, and then it'd be morning. That night I didn't think it would ever be morning as I listened to my dad walking round and round on the hardwood floor downstairs in his blue leather cowboy boots.

three

But you have to get up

Morning came anyway. It was grey, it was snowing. I ate some stale blackberry pie for breakfast and I left out my dad's teacup with a Lipton's teabag in it. I left through the front door and, passing through the living room, I saw that chipped-up bulldog sitting on the coffee table—just sitting there with its painted pink tongue hanging out.

When I got out by the mailbox, Richie Levy was already there waiting for the bus. I was cold—I only had a sweater on. The snow was like glue, how it stuck to your face, your eyelashes. The pie kept rolling around in my stomach.

While we were waiting for the school bus, Richie gave me a roll of caps to explode at recess. Richie and I both knew that he wouldn't ever bang those black dots with a rock to make explosions, I would. I'd probably get caught and have to go stand in the coat closet, but I didn't care. Richie was always trying to live in my body, but that day I didn't even say anything mean. Richie never minded if I was mean because nobody else but me would talk to him at school. There aren't many Jewish people in Clermont County and there aren't too many daughters of hog farmers, either. I suppose we could have gotten away with being Jewish or raising hogs if we'd been pretty looking or good at sports. Anyway, I wasn't always mean—sometimes I was nice.

Richie was always trying to teach me about Jewishness by pointing out that Jewish people were chosen. Which made me not chosen. "We are God's chosen people." It did worry me some, but I didn't stop to think then, chosen for what?

Richie lived next door to us but he lived in the housing development. The Levys' house was just over our creek. It was brand new, had sliding glass doors and a garbage disposal. Mr. Levy said they were going to put a swimming pool in, but they never did.

Rachel and Diane were Richie's older sisters. They were older than me and so stuck-up that I always told Richie they were going to get nose sprains. Rachel had braces on her top and bottom teeth. I liked to look her over at the bus stop and get her all squirmy, then I'd wait until she opened her mouth to say something and I'd say, "Cornflakes." I like to think that took her down a peg or two. But that day, with the pie in my stomach like to kill me and my momma gone Lord knows where, Richie said, "Flu bug. They're home throwing up their guts."

Richie was a creep, no question, but I didn't know anyone else with a garbage disposal and the possibility of a swimming pool. On our farm was a pond that was scummy at the time of year you most wanted to swim in it, filled with things you couldn't see in the muddy water—snapping turtles that'd take your toes off soon as look at you and maybe cottonmouths just waiting to wind their way around you. As far as garbage goes, anything edible we gave to the hogs. I slopped them every morning after breakfast, every night after dinner. Hogs'll eat anything but are particularly fond of egg shells and orange rinds. If we had a garbage disposal we'd grind everything up, leaving nothing for the hogs who'd have to root for acorns and starve to death. I was with my momma when it came to not liking living with hogs.

No bus still. I stomped my feet to get the cold out.

"Hey! Did you see *Psycho* yet?" Richie said. "They showed that part, you know"—he tried to stab me with his ruler, but I knocked it out of his hand— "where he gets her in the shower. Man!" Richie's face was all lit up. "Lots of blood really comes out, lots of blood."

I got to give it to Richie, sometimes he could feel my mood. I knew he was trying hard to cheer me up.

"We watched Red Skelton, then my mom left again." Richie was throwing rocks at the blackbirds on the cyclone fence. He was missing. He always missed. "Yeah? Where'd she go this time?"

We saw the bus coming, orange and black through the snow and when Hal stopped for us, he made sure to stop right in front of the biggest, slushiest puddle in the road.

"This time she's gone for good," I said as I stepped up onto the bus.

"How do you know?"

"I just do. She's probably dead already in a ditch."

"Wow," said Richie. I told him to shut up and I gave him a look to help him do it.

"Mornin' miss miss missy," said Hal, the bus driver, spit all gummed up on the side of his mouth.

"Yech," I said.

We sat down behind Hal on the hard vinyl seats.

Richie and me, to keep ourselves going, always made fun of Hal. We'd wrench up our faces to look as retarded as possible, sitting there behind Hal's driver's seat, and every kid who got on the bus would get a performance.

Sandy Shaw got on the bus. Nothing different, nothing new, like I said, this was practically a tradition, when Hal turns around suddenly and smacks me across the face but good, slams on the brakes, opens the door to the bus, and tells me to get out.

Richie Levy sunk into his seat and acted like he never did anything wrong, wouldn't look at me. Silence. Nobody said a word. Hal was aiming eyeball pitchforks at me so I stood up, my lip bleeding where he smacked me, and walked down the steps of the bus into the snow and he just drove away.

I stood there awhile. I was only about a quarter of a mile away from home, but I didn't think it was such a good thing to be going back there, my dad and all. I knew he'd be worked up. So I set off walking to school. Wasn't that far, a few miles. Where else was there to go?

By the time I pulled open the side door at school my lip had stopped bleeding. I could hear the Pledge of Allegiance over the loudspeaker. I stood in the hallway, waiting for it to end before I went into Mr. Sanders' class. Mr. Martin was doing his hall patrol—making sure nobody like me was cutting out on the Pledge. As soon as he saw me a look came over him: his face puckered up like he'd swallowed something sour, then he smiled, and a shiver went up me. I bit my lip, opened up that wound, and tasted blood.

"Isobel?"

I walked over to the door of Mr. Sanders' class, like I didn't hear him. All eyes swung over to me. I licked the blood off my lip.

"Isobel! In my office, *now*," Mr. Martin's voice boomed behind me and into the classroom. There were some giggles from the class. I heard Mr. Sanders tell everyone to calm down. I closed the door and followed Mr. Martin, who was rubbing his hands together, down the hallway to his office.

Mr. Martin's office was painted light green—made me think of food-colored eggs at Easter. Dusty old pull blinds covered up the windows and only tiny bits of light managed to sneak through. I felt underwater.

"Park yourself in that chair there, Isobel." There was snow on Mr. Martin's brown suit jacket. I looked closer and saw it was some of the biggest dandruff flakes in the world. "You know, some people are not as bright as others." Mr. Martin rubbed his hands together till he saw me watching. He took out a handkerchief and dried them off. I looked over his head at the calendar. First Bank of Morseville was advertised on it. Mr. Potter, who taught me in Sunday school, was standing out front of the bank waving in a picture, and everyone who worked for him was out there waving too.

"Hal Szyerkowski tells me you were cutting up on his bus, acting up, making fun."

"He clobbered me!"

"Isobel, Isobel. My word, child, don't you know some people have problems? We don't make fun of people with problems. Now, Hal's a bit slow ..."

"Retarded, you mean."

Mr. Martin slammed a hand down on his desk, boom! Dust flew and hung up there in the green, underwater air. "That's it, that's it. I'm at the end of my rope."

I looked back at the calendar—did Mr. Potter make his whole staff stand outside every month? Were they still waving in June?

I smiled at him—like I had dimples. "Sorry," says me.

I'm really going to have to call your mother he says, I really don't know what to do with you, he says, we're going to have to take *some* kind of *action,* he says.

"My mother's not home."

"Your father, then."

"Not home."

"Well," he says, "what kind of impression, just *what* kind of impression do you think you are making on the other kids, the little ones?"

Of course I hoped it was a rotten one, but I didn't say it. I just kept up the smiling.

"The library," said Mr. Martin, eyes beetling into me, boring into me. "Take your lunch, you did bring your lunch?"

I nodded. I had my Woody Woodpecker lunchbox with nothing in it.

"Take your lunch and spend the day in the library. No talking, no recess."

I stood up, the back of my skirt sticking to my legs from the hard wooden chair I'd been sitting in. "And, Isobel"—he began to rub his hands together—"think about those who are less fortunate."

"He popped me in the mouth!"

"The library." Mr. Martin and me stared at each other, but I finally won. He picked up some paper off his desk and started scribbling on it. I slammed his door good and hard on the way out.

four

Where I was when it happened

I walked down the hallway to the library, my shoes sounding hollow, myself feeling empty. I did actually think about some less fortunates. The lady in the shower scene in *Psycho* was less fortunate than me. Richie Levy was less fortunate because he was a total creep, a chicken liver, and also Jewish. People said when I asked them why they didn't like Richie or his family it was because they killed Christ, which is ridiculous because Christ has been dead for at least five million years. OK, not five million because there were dinosaurs then but far back, way too far back for the Levys to have been involved, but still, people didn't like them. Then there was my dad, he was less fortunate because he loved my mom, Clematis, to death. But look at this, this is what I figured: my mom, Clematis, would surely die, either in a car crash or drinking or something; my dad, who couldn't take it without her would kill himself and *then* nobody would be less fortunate than *me* because I would be an orphan. And nobody wants an orphan.

I pushed open the glass door to the library. On the door a poster with a pink elephant was saying, *Read the Adventure!* Miss Lytle was picking at her blue angora sweater when I came in. She didn't say anything, just looked over her glasses at me. I sat down on an orange plastic chair and picked up one of the books piled up on the reading table, *Virginia*

Dare—Lost Daughter of Roanoke. I scanned. This girl was dumb enough to do everything she was told not to do and got kidnapped by Indians and vanished. They figure she either got scalped or raised by these Indians, but they didn't know. They just made stuff up to make it sound like Virginia was brave.

I was kind of daydreaming, sitting there, branches outside scraping against the windows. Miss Lytle was sneaking a cigarette behind her desk like I couldn't see her. It was very dark outside—I pictured my momma dead in her coffin. She was beautiful (of course, always, and she couldn't help it and said she hated it, but I never believed her), she had pink tiger lilies on her breast, and she was smiling. I had on my green velvet dress she'd bought me last spring. I was crying—silently, no sniffling. I was crying like a saint.

A voice came over the loudspeaker. "Is this on?" Tapping sounds boomed in the air. "Children and faculty, I ..." Mr. Martin's voice faded away.

A high whine suddenly came blasting out of the speaker. I plugged up my ears and looked at Miss Lytle who didn't plug her ears, but looked like she wanted to. "Point it away from the speaker. No, the other way." That was Mrs. Snowden, school secretary. We heard Mr. Martin clear his throat. "May I have silence, please. This is confirmed? Who did it? What?" Miss Lytle and me looked at each other. We already were silent. "Children and faculty, we have just heard, been informed, of some terrible, terrible news. Today, in Dallas, Texas, our President, Mr. John F. Kennedy, was shot in the head."

Miss Lytle made a dog-trapped rabbit sound and covered up her mouth with her hand. She looked at me. I shrugged.

Mr. Martin's voice came back on. "Is he dead? Huh? Alright, he's not dead, but it's very serious. I think we should have a prayer for his recovery. Each of you pray to yourselves for five minutes. OK Samantha, shut me off here. Is this off? Serves him right, I say … Is this off? (Coughing.) Children, pray!'' The loudspeaker made a sound like wind caught in a rain barrel.

five

That little girl

The President of the United States shot, then dead. I got home and my dad was alive, hadn't hung himself or stabbed himself or anything and I figured that was pretty good. I can't tell you how he usually carries on when my momma leaves. But he was like a zombie. I figured that it was better he was living dead than dead dead.

On the news we found out JFK had died. All my dad said is the country is going to hell in a handbasket. I did do some praying. I felt it was my duty; I mean, he was the President, but I guess I'd used up all my prayer power to keep my dad from killing himself over Clematis.

There was no school the day of the funeral so we sat in front of the TV and watched the ceremony. I fixed us hamburgers and we ate them on the TV trays with the pressed-in butterflies. I watched him to make sure he ate and he did, and drank three beers. There were so many people at that funeral, and horses! It was very beautiful, horses with black feathers. I saw the kids, his kids, holding their mom's hand. She had a black veil on so I couldn't see her face. I figured they'd be kicked out of the White House now. I felt sorry for those kids. They looked so lost, especially the little girl. She was holding on to her mother's hand for dear life.

Now, they were less fortunate then me. Maybe. They'd lost one, I'd lost one, but it looked like I might be losing another one any time now. I knew they didn't have pigs that broke out of their pen and sniffed and snuffed around their screen door at night. Those kids probably had horses—maybe some of those with the feathers.

But I'll tell you. I never saw anything so grand as that funeral. I never saw so many people crying at once. I knew the little girl, his girl, would be afraid to go to sleep that night. I knew just how she felt.

six

A story

My dad is named Prince Roundtree. He's not really the prince of anything, it's just his name. He has told me many stories, some maybe true, about our family. My favorite story is about my great grandmother who I saw dying when I was about five years old. The way I saw her dying was that my dad took me to her house to say goodbye to her. I thought this was sad because I never remembered even saying hello.

One day, my dad and me were sitting outside breaking string beans into a bushel basket. It was a time when my momma was around, hadn't been drinking or wandering off in the middle of the day, and she was feeling love for us. She brought us fresh-squeezed lemonade and a radio out under the walnut tree where we were sitting on matching lawn chairs.

My momma pulled up a chair and tuned the radio to a station that was playing an Elvis Presley record. She fanned herself with a magazine and sipped lemonade through a straw while my dad told me about how my great grandmother came to be a healer and what happened when she met The Riders of the Dark Night.

My dad kept breaking beans with rhythm and regularity while he talked and every once in awhile my momma fanned the back of my neck where the sweat was tangling up in my hair. Every so often while my dad was talking, she'd hum the tune to the song on the radio softly to herself.

I looked up from my beans.

"Your great grandma's name was Beatrice and she had some blue, blue eyes, I'll tell you, like the clearest day or probably like an ocean looks where it laps up against a tropical island. When I was a boy she could charm me like a snake with those blue eyes of hers."

I remembered my great grandma that time I'd seen her, the mummy woman lying in bed dying, staring at me with those very same eyes. "Goodbye," I'd said softly. Her hand had been soft as snapdragon petals.

"Was she beautiful when she was young?" I asked.

"No, she wasn't beautiful, leastways not from her photographs. She had this beak here like mine, but she was unusual looking and very strong." He grabbed a lapful of beans from the basket and I watched as his fingers seemed to blur and the beans jumped into the waiting bushel basket.

"In fact," started my dad. My momma stopped fanning my neck and got up and rubbed the back of my dad's neck, rubbed his arms some, too. He smiled up at her in a way that made me think of a dog getting his tummy rubbed.

"In fact," I said loud.

"In fact," said my dad now that my momma sat back down and started reading a movie magazine, "she was so strong it was almost like a legend up in the hills where she lived with her daddy and brothers. She was the only girl."

"Yeah?" I'd forgotten about the beans and my dad scooped up a big handful and dropped them onto the newspaper on my lap. I started snapping them— their hollow pops will stay in my ears forever.

"Yeah. One time?" My dad threw some bad beans in the discard pile for the hogs and reached for another handful to break up. "An uncle told me this.

One time Beatrice's dad, that would be your great great grandpa, got stuck under a fallen horse."

"Why didn't the horse get up?"

"I don't know, maybe it died or something."

"Why did it die?"

"I don't know, Isobel—heat stroke—maybe it wasn't dead. Honey, where you goin'?" My momma was standing up and looking across the cornfield.

"Nowhere," she said to the corn. She looked back at my dad and smiled. "Nowhere, sweetie, finish your story."

"Well," said my dad, "Beatrice saw her dad go down and she shot out to the road like a bolt of lightning and heaved that horse off him, lifted the damn horse clean off him and then threw her daddy over her shoulder. This uncle said he was a big man, too—over two hundred pounds. She carried him a quarter mile up to the house and set his broken leg."

"Muscles," I said. I was picturing great grandmother Roundtree looking like Charles Atlas, but with longer hair. "Wow."

"But before that she lived in a convent."

"She was a nun?"

"Nope, she wanted to be, but they said she didn't have the calling. She married Jerome Roundtree, your great grandpa."

My father smiled at my mother and she smiled back. I had stopped with my pile of beans for now and held my hair up off the back of my neck, waiting for that cool breeze from my mother.

"Now your great grandma told me herself she was a pain in the butt."

"What do you mean a pain in the butt?"

"She talked back to everyone. Couldn't keep her mouth shut, never could keep her opinions to herself. She acted like she was smarter than anybody else. That, she believed, was the main reason they wouldn't let her be a nun. They said she didn't have the calling, but she thought it was because she never learned meekness."

"Like me?"

"Like you what?"

"A pain in the butt!" My mom and dad laughed. Oh, they laughed together on that August afternoon, in the heat, in the shade, music going, birds drowsing in the trees. I smiled at them, proud of them for being so beautiful.

"Yeah, a lot like you," my dad said. My momma was quietly singing, and she bent her head toward the radio.

"Up there in the convent—she was there about six months—she got her hands on a book about the life of Saint Joan. She said that changed her life, that's what gave her the calling. Saint Joan of Arc became her pipeline to God. But the nuns in the convent didn't take to her telling them how to get better yield in their fields, or how to properly butcher a cow, or how to hoe a row of turnips. They sent her packing back to her daddy's farm.

"Well, back home she started praying a lot. She laid out in the center of a road with her arms and legs out like she was nailed to a cross waiting for a sign, or a wagon to run her over. She starved herself till she weighed next to nothing. She lived out in a hut with no heat in the winter. Everyone thought she was just plain nuts. And at twenty-four her hair turned completely white—not grey, but long and winter white. Her hair hadn't never been cut since she was a baby.

"Now seems there was an Indian man in those parts who'd lost his entire family to influenza. Nobody knows how he and Beatrice happened to end up together. One day she just turned up at her father's farm—her brothers are all there eating breakfast and in waltzes their crazy sister—eyes so blue you could dive in and swim—with this Indian, this Cherokee named Roundtree."

"My great grandpa was a real Indian?"

"Cherokee. Her daddy almost gets an attack when he finds out that that's her husband, almost falls down dead of a heart attack."

"Why?"

"Didn't like Indians."

"Why?"

"So they run them off, the brothers and the father, they run Beatrice and her Indian fellow off the farm and told them, 'Don't come back if you know what's good for you!' They left, see, and the Indian ..."

"My great grandpa ..."

"Yeah, he had some land up on top of a little mountain, rocky soil, not much good for anything, but that's what they had. A baby was born in the summer, but it died by Christmas."

"How sad," I said, beans forgotten. Even my momma looked sad. She stroked my cheek with the back of her hand, she tucked some stray hairs back behind my ear. My dad patted my momma's knee and she took her hand away from me and leaned into him, moved her chair closer, and leaned her head on his shoulder. He closed his eyes. The beans lay on my dad's lap now, and his hands thrummed the aluminum arms of the lawnchair in time to the music on the radio. My momma hummed.

"So what happened?" I said loudly as my dad reached over and stroked my momma's hair, that hair that looked like it was burning in the sun.

My momma was singing pretty loud with Jerry Lee Lewis and didn't seem to notice us anymore. She'd lifted her head up off my dad's shoulder and was singing louder and louder, singing to the corn and singing to the clouds in the sky.

31

My dad was staring at her with that lost in the wilderness face he got sometimes. She hummed some of the words she didn't know. I wanted to kick her radio clean across the yard. Just like her, just like her.

I got up and sat on my daddy's lap. I sat right on the pile of beans and he shoved me off.

"I want to know what happened then, Daddy. What happened?" I sat back down in my lawn chair.

"So they lived up there a few years."

My momma was living her own fast life in her head right then and we both knew it. My momma was singing on stage with Jerry Lee Lewis, but this time my dad went on talking to me.

"Make a long story short, she lost the bloom she'd put on when she married Roundtree. She lost her calling from God. She never baked, never chopped more wood than was needed, and they hardly ever spoke—she and her husband. They lived. That's what they did and every day was the same. Until something happened that changed your great grandma's life forever."

"What?"

"What happened was that one evening, along about twilight, your great grandma was out doing something in the barn, settling the stock or whatever, and suddenly she hears a sound like thunder coming right up through the fields. She looked out the barn door and saw something like twenty men on horseback all dressed up in black with black scarves tied over their faces. It was The Riders of the Dark Night.

"First thing she thought when she saw them was, didn't they look silly? But then she got worried because she could see they were coming for a reason and it didn't look like a good one.

"Now, she'd never seen them riding before, but she'd heard enough about them to know how they hated everyone but their own and she'd heard a gruesome story about how they'd strung up a poor Negro man with barbed wire just a couple of months before.

"So she peeked out of the barn and saw them go straight into the little house, five or so of them, and drag her husband out into the yard in his longjohns. Then they punched her husband until he lay still on the ground. They had him lying there on the ground and two of 'em commenced war whooping around him in a circle.

"Now she didn't know what to do. She stood there in that dark barn, watching her husband curled up on the ground, screaming out words in Cherokee. She said she started to shake and then something just came over her. She thought of Saint Joan, the picture she'd seen in her book, riding into battle with a halo around her head and she said it came to her as a vision, filled with light around the edges and the only reason she didn't stop to drop down on her knees and hear the holy angels sing was because they were just then throwing a rope around a limb of the maple tree.

"And that's when she knew what she had to do."

"What, Daddy?" I said, my bean pile forgotten on my lap. Even Momma was bending near to hear.

"Well," said my daddy, "she pulled her hair out of the braid she kept it in and it came down to the back of her knees. Then she got some matches from the place they kept them in the barn and threw a bridle on the plow horse. She tore off her clothes and jumped on the horse, dumped some kerosene on her hair, set her hair on fire, and crashed out of the barn—right through the rotted wood—with a cry coming out of her that must have sounded like twenty wild Indians.

"When those hellish men caught sight of her— this big woman naked on a horse with an orange halo of fire, screaming a war cry—they scrambled to their horses. And they rode away without even a goodbye and that was the end of them."

"Didn't she burn up?"

"She got burned bad. She threw herself into the pig trough as soon as they were down the road apiece and that saved her life. There's a good reason to have hogs, don't you think? She would of burned to death if that pig trough hadn't been there. But she did get awful burnt up. Had those horrible scars all over her face and neck till the day she died. But, you know, no one ever called her ugly. See, she had a special something that just glowed out from the inside of her like the sun."

"A holy miracle like in the Bible," I said, thinking how she could of died in a minute, burned up like a newspaper thrown into a fire.

"I think it was more that she dived into water before her skin burned completely off."

"I think it was a miracle," I said.

"Who knows?" said my dad. "But it was after that she began to heal by hand. Just touching and healing. People came and got healed and even some scientists from New York City came to test her healing. But that's another story."

It was getting to be twilight. Bats and swallows dipped for bugs in the purple-streaked sky. My dad took my momma by the hand and they went off walking, the radio between them. After awhile I couldn't see them anymore. I could just hear the music coming in crystal clear in the evening air.

"Beatrice Roundtree," I said to the darkening sky. "I wish I could heal."

seven

Our place

Some people need the land as bad as they need skin. The Prince is like that. Needs his land under his feet and needs to know when he's walking it that it's his. Anyway, the land is a skin really, the skin that covers up all the earth's insides. Maybe I need land, too. Maybe that came down to me from my dad because I can feel it beating underneath my feet in the cornfields.

Our farm was bought by my grandpa, great grandma Roundtree's son. After the one that died she had one that lived. We raise feed corn, soybeans, alfalfa, and hogs. My dad would like to have nothing but hogs. Hogs and land. He doesn't have the particular need to grow anything on the land, just hogs. You should see my dad in the fall, how he gets, all sad and down. Fall is butchering time and we have to sell stock and it's got to be killed. I don't particularly like hogs but I don't like seeing them killed either.

The Prince loads them up himself and talks to them, each of them as they make their way up the ramp, sometimes with a bucket on the head and them walking backwards trying to get it off. My dad sweet-talks them and puts on a brave face. "They can tell, Issy, they can feel it." My dad spends the rest of that day in the barn with Elmo, his prize hog, and doesn't eat any pork for a week or two.

But since his daddy planted the land my daddy feels it is his responsibility to continue the planting so he puts in the crops, rotating when he's supposed to,

35

and harvests and sells what he's got. I help.

I learned to drive a tractor when I was nine. I've got long legs and strong arms and I can shift the gears fine. I get brown and smell like sweat and bug spray out in the fields. I sleep fine all night long after helping my dad.

I don't do it alone. Help plant and harvest, I mean. We have men and boys who come, some for a share of feed corn, some for a few dollars. Fred Emery came just for fun till he died a couple of years ago. He was Prince's best friend.

I'll tell you how it was that last summer he was here when we were putting up corn and you might get a picture of what our place is like.

Our house is almost a hundred years old. It sits down in a little bit of a valley from the gravel road that leads to Express Highway 70. We got trees around the house that might be old as Daniel Boone. That's what Fred Emery used to tell me. "Old as Dan'l Boone, those trees, uncommonly big." Elms.

Our house hasn't been painted since I was a baby in diapers, but it used to be white. That summer it looked mostly grey under the shade of the trees. It was a box house—two stories and built like a box. There was a front porch with some trimming carved around it.

From my window in the front of the house I could climb onto a branch of the biggest elm and sit there at night, watch the lightning bugs, and count the stars.

Our land spreads out on three sides. My grandpa didn't buy past the creek to the east where Cornwall Commons, the housing development, sits now. We've got three hundred acres, mostly good soil, and we got a woods.

My dad doesn't hold with trespassers, hunters, or bums wandering through. He's got a shotgun behind the door of his bedroom, double barrel, and it'll take the head off of anything. He takes it sometimes, into a twilight, over the rise from the house. He just goes and checks the land and makes sure there aren't any trespassers. He doesn't let me come.

The last summer Fred Emery was with us was as good a summer as ever was. Clematis wasn't drinking and was attending church regularly. I was doing Sunday school with Mr. Potter. Fred used to come over Sundays, after we got back from church, and Prince and him would sit up on the porch and drink beer and Wild Turkey until their sentences started to get twisty and tangled. Then they'd just sit and sit and not say a word. They'd just look out at the land and watch the sun come down.

Fred treated me more like a boy than a girl and I appreciated that. He didn't sweet-talk me or try to talk about things I didn't care about anyway—dolls or dresses or anything. When he and my dad got going and started telling their stories he never curbed anything because I was there.

One summer evening, must of been about July because it wasn't too humid like August and it stayed light a pretty long time, Fred was over and he and my dad were sitting on the porch. Clematis was sitting behind me on the porch swing and I was kneeling down in front of her getting my hair french-braided. She kissed the part in my hair and called me a sugar bunny.

I could see the barn, looking out ahead of me, and I could see the sky turning purple-pink. Behind the barn were the woods and spreading out to the woods was corn. There was a wind, and the leaves fluttered like golden ribbons where the last sun hit them. I was just about the happiest I'd ever been. Then I heard Fred Emery crying.

At first I thought he'd got something caught

down in his throat, but his face was working, twitching and all, and then there were tears crashing down his face. He was crying hard.

"Now, Fred," said my dad.

"What's the matter, Fred?" asked my mom. He didn't say anything, just sat there, a hand spread out on each knee. He was big. Bigger than my dad by far. Not fat, but big, and people were afraid of him. I wasn't. But we knew him. Still, you didn't expect to see someone like that start crying like a baby.

"Freddy?" said my dad.

He turned to us, my mom and me. "Did you ever?" He held his arms up like he was hugging the sky to him. "Lord, it's a beautiful world."

We looked out and we all saw it, too. Saw it different. The sky was just a certain shade of rose and gold, the clouds seemed painted on by God. A beam of light came out of the clouds and danced on the barn and made it glow.

My dad put his hand on Fred's and patted it. My momma smiled and pulled me to her.

It was a beautiful world. And all I knew of the world, really, was our farm, so our farm was the world.

Fred dried his eyes with the back of his hand, sniffled some. He smiled at me.

Fred died a bit later—car crash. He died quick and didn't suffer. He didn't have any family so we did the funeral, the laying out and all and the burying. My dad paid to have a granite headstone put up. It doesn't have anything but the name and the date he died. He's planning to put more one day, he says, it just hasn't come to him what yet.

Can you see the land? If you see it through Fred's eyes, you've seen our place.

I think we should just put IT'S A BEAUTIFUL WORLD on the headstone. Even if it isn't true always, through

Fred's eyes it was. I wish I could always have eyes to see like that.

eight

The Cat Man and finding Clematis

The note said that she was fine, that she didn't have a telephone. That's how the Prince and me found out that Clematis was living in Terre Sacre and singing in a nightclub.

By now she'd been gone about five months and spring was floating up by way of the morning glories outside my window. It was a particularly warm spring, already the air was moist and sweet. Some nights were warm enough to dance a hula.

We were getting along pretty good without Clematis. It was, though, the longest time she'd ever left us.

The Prince talked to himself a lot and still got that look in his eyes several times a day. I'd give him a cup of coffee in the morning and off he'd go. I'd see it as the steam wrapped up around his mustache and then snuck up his nose. His eyes would empty out of living soul and leave me just an empty husk of a dad.

He managed to feed the hogs, pack some off for spring auction over at J. Shire's, and fill up our freezer with meat for the summer. I didn't go with him this time. He put in a few crops, some beans, feed corn, and alfalfa, but I'd see him out there with the spreader, sometimes going round and round in a circle, digging himself in and getting nowhere.

I'd put away most of Clematis's things that she kept laying around. I'd wrapped the china dog up in

41

tissue paper and put it in a box. The other doodads she laid around everywhere I'd collected and put in a trunk down in the root cellar.

I was going to put her clothes in the trunk, too, but the Prince caught me at it and closed the door to the cedar closet. He snatched the black silk dress right out of my hands and told me to get the hell out of his room.

The day the note came in the mail I knew something was up. I came back from school and my dad was on his knees scrubbing the brown and yellow linoleum squares in the kitchen.

She was on her way back. I knew it. My stomach turned my lunch into a hot burning juice that kept trying to get up my throat. The Prince was humming to himself. I'd never heard my dad sing or even hum, not even in church. I had always figured he had a real bad voice, but he was humming real pretty.

"Hey," I said.

"Hey, punkin," he said.

"That floor's pretty dirty."

"Sure is."

The grey water in the plastic bucket smelled of vinegar. In the bucket were some dead beetles and lots of hair that had tangled up in knots. These things floated on the top of the water. I wondered for a minute how all that hair got on the kitchen floor. But Clematis always dried her hair out by the wood stove here. Everywhere, everywhere was a piece of her.

My dad's hands on the mop showed big thick veins filled in with blue. I sat down at the kitchen table and lifted up my feet so he could mop around the table legs.

"How come you're mopping the floor today?" I asked. I had never ever seen him mop the floor on any day. The way he did it—one stab with the mop to the right, then another to the left—showed that he knew more about shoveling manure.

"Had a letter from your mom today." He scraped with his thumbnail at a stubborn spot near the refrigerator. "She's up to Terre Sacre. She's singing in a nightclub."

I sat there still and held my knees to my cheek.

"I figure we'll run up there this evening and surprise her at her show, maybe."

"How come?"

"How come! How come! Because we want to see her, want to know she's OK, because we want to bring her home to a nice clean house. How come. How can you ask how come?"

"If she wanted a nice clean house she could come here and clean it herself."

My dad hit me. He slapped my leg right above the knee where my shorts ended. He didn't hit me hard—it just stung and glowed pink. He could have hurt me, could have slugged me good. I got up and tracked up his clean floor.

"You wash up," he said. "Wash up and clean your room."

I stood on the back stoop and looked at him through the screen door. He turned his back to me and remopped where I'd walked. He wasn't humming now. He knew I was watching him so I left and went around to the front door and sat on the porch.

I had always wanted a porch swing. We had these heavy red metal chairs with rockers built in. They call them gliders. They sat out in all weather, so they were pitted and rusty. In these chairs your hair got caught by the rusted metal and pulled out of your head when you got up. They also screeched when you tried to rock. I was screeching when a car pulled down the driveway. Looked like a nice car, but dirty. Big black Cadillac.

The car pulled right past the gravel onto the

grass. A man got out. He was about my dad's age, I guess, real tall, red-headed.

"Hey, hey, little lady." He was smoking a cigarette down to the end. I sat up in my rusty rocker and got my hair caught and some of it pulled out. "Your momma about?"

"Who're you?" I didn't think I liked his easy way just coming right up and resting one foot on the porch, looking right into my face.

"I'm your mother's cousin and I brought you something. What do you think it is?" I didn't know my momma had any cousins around where we lived. In fact, she said she didn't have anybody, anywhere.

I looked him over and he wasn't hiding anything behind his back. Whatever he had brought me couldn't be too much.

"What is it?" I put my legs together, then took them down off the porch railing. He was looking around, looking in the windows.

"Your daddy home?"

"What is it?"

"You're something, aren't you? Now, here you go, reach in my pocket here and see what you find." He came up close to me and turned so that I could reach right in and see what was there. I did. I could feel the sweat off him through the pocket lining, but I felt some paper and I pulled out a dollar bill.

"There you go."

"My mom's not here."

"I'll talk to your dad."

I looked at him then and his eyes were cat's-eye green.

"He isn't here."

"Well, that's kinda funny, him leaving you here all alone with evening just creepin' up. All alone out here in the country." He looked around, then started whistling. I felt like he was measuring something, adding something up in his head.

"What's so funny? I'm not scared. My best friend lives right over there in Cornwall Commons." I pointed to the housing development that started right at the edge of our big side yard, pointed specifically at Richie Levy's window. "I could just run, you know, and scream real loud and everybody over there would come running out of their houses to see what was wrong with me."

He looked over to where the first ranch house sat—three quarters of an acre or so on the other side of the creek—and spit on one of his shoes.

Me, on the other hand, I watched him sharp. Looking back over at the Levys' I knew I couldn't count on much—most I'd hope for if I screamed was that my dad would come running out with his shot-gun or Richie would look out his window and call the sheriff.

But he went to his car and sat on the driver's side seat and got out a rag and polished his shoe. I don't know why. His shoes weren't nice shoes, just old brown things. I hoped my dad wouldn't come out of the house. I hoped he couldn't hear anything. I wanted this man to just go away and never know my dad. He was a cat man, this man. He could scratch you deep.

He watched me some more from his car, his door open, him lounging in his seat, and lit up another cigarette. "OK there, Matilda. OK, I'll go. But I'll be back because I got business with your daddy. You tell him that a man came in a great big ol' black Caddy to give him the news. No, better make that the blues, babydoll." He leaned on his car door.

"What's your name?" I looked him in the eye.

He looked me right back and said, "Tell your momma Johnnie Pearl's out and I've come for her." He winked at me. "You tell her that, Matilda."

I was going to ask him what he meant, but he slammed the car door shut and spun the tires, waking up dust and flinging gravel.

"My name's not Matilda!" I yelled at the fins of the Cadillac.

He turned onto the road when the Prince slammed the front screen door closed behind him.

"Who's that?"

"Salesman," I lied.

"What was he selling?"

"Cats," I told him.

"Cats?"

"And Bibles. He was selling Bibles and he'd give you a free kitten if you bought one. I told him we were Jewish."

My dad came and sat down in the other rusty rocker and fanned himself with his John Deere cap. "Oooh, boy. Hot."

I hardly listened. I sat there in my rocker and I knew that cat man would come back.

"Go clean yourself up. We'll stop at the Dairy Queen on our way to Terre Sacre."

I stood up and he patted me on the fanny. I went up to my room and picked out my prettiest babydoll dress and my black Shirley Temple shoes.

When I met him by the truck he was wearing his good corduroys and a white shirt I'd never seen before. He held open my door for me.

We listened to the Midwestern Hayride on the radio on the way over to the Dairy Queen. The sun was sneaking away and the sky was summer pink and blue. Bats flew zigzags across the sky.

I think that was for me and him one of the happiest private evenings—that night we drove the two hours up to Terre Sacre. We shared a DQ sundae after burgers and Cokes. I remember hearing Porter Wagoner and the Wagonmasters coming in so clear in the cab of the truck singing "Tom Dooley."

We barreled along, winding through the evening toward Clematis.

"Sweet Sal, you're my gal," sang the voice of a lonesome cowboy to my dad and me.

"Now, this here's music." The Prince smiled some love my way. "It's gonna all work out, Issy."

I didn't say anything.

nine

She sings and dances

We had never been up to Terre Sacre. I guess because we didn't have a reason. I don't think the Prince had ever been there either because he didn't know where to go when we got there. It sat up on the Ohio River like a sideshow.

We drove down the main street. It was called Center Avenue. All the streets smelled like water. I smelled it strong, the river, because I'd never smelled a river like that before. Off to the side we passed Beechnut, Pine, Elm, Sycamore, and Spruce. Then started Buchanan, Arthur, Wilson, Eisenhower. I read them off to the Prince.

"What street do we want, Daddy?"

"I don't really know. She didn't say."

"How're we gonna find it then?"

"We'll smell it out."

"Jefferson, Jackson," I sang.

"Quiet, I'm huntin'," said my dad. The farther into town we drove, the farther apart the buildings got. Lights sparkled, colors running up and down. *JOEY'S BABYDOLL LOUNGE—REAL DOLLS.*

"I don't see any signs that say nightclub," I said.

Terre Sacre is known as Sin City. I'd heard people joking about it. I knew they had dance places there.

My dad was in the Lions Club and they had dances, too, so I guess he just ignored Terre Sacre. I'd danced with my dad at the Lions Club Hall. He swirled me around in my green velvet dress till my skirt stood straight out around me.

But he was picturing a nightclub here in Sin City just like me, I bet. One of those places from a Fred Astaire movie. Black, white, and silver with a long, winding staircase to move down slowly, singing.

"Let's pull in here," said the Prince as we swung into a bank parking lot. Across the street was a bar with neon martini glasses that tilted and winked at me.

He got out of the truck and looked up the street. A liquor store called *L's* had a bright pink electric sign.

"I'm going over to that store there. You stay put."

"I'm coming."

"Stay put."

He walked off toward *L's* fiery light.

I yanked open the Chevy door and snuck off after him. I tracked him and peeked around the edge of the glass door at my dad inside talking to a fat man. The fat man had a hairy stomach. My dad glanced over at the door and saw my sneaky little head. He came over to the door, pulled it open, and snatched me inside before I knew what I was about. He held me by the hand.

"As I was saying, you ever heard of Clematis Roundtree?"

The fat man behind the counter was staring at my dad, then me, then back up to my dad.

"Who?" he asked.

"Where's the best nightclub around here?" asked my dad.

The man whose belly peeked out of his shirt right at the bellybutton said, "What're you looking for?" and looked back down to me again.

My dad put his arm around my shoulder. "Looking for my wife."

He shook his head and shook his belly too and

turned away. "Shit," said the man.

"I kindly ask you to watch your mouth."

"What you want her for?" The man turned back around and leaned on his hairy elbows and eyed me good.

I felt my dad's hand clench up on my collar. I smelled that sweat on him I smelled when he punched Limmie Ryan's dad in the nose for saying something that I didn't hear to my mom.

"This here is my daughter and I would appreciate it if you would mind your manners."

I stared into the man's eyes. One didn't move when the other one did. One eye fixed on me and the other eye stayed right where it was. The one that stayed was pale blue. The other was brown as dirt.

"Listen, mister, it's your business and all, but I can't see why you'd be takin' a child into one of these places." My dad's ears started turning pink.

"Don't read me a book on how to bring up my child, friend. Her mother is a singer and we've come to take her home."

The man leaned over the counter next to the cash register. "Can I see you a minute?" he said to my dad. "Here, girlie, have a Milky Way."

I took the candy, but I didn't eat it.

I watched them talking by the Jack Daniels bottles.

The Prince twitched and I thought he'd hit the fat man.

I leaned in.

"There's a new gal over to the Black Magic Club." The fat man looked toward me. He lowered his voice and I couldn't hear anything else.

They stared at each other, eyes caught on each other.

Before I could say anything, my dad was dragging me out of that liquor store by the right arm. His hand clamped down on my wrist felt worse than an Indian rope burn. The toes of my shoes made long scrapes in the gravel on the way to the truck.

My dad had that lost-in-the-wilderness look. "No," I said.

"Yes," he said. Quiet and he meant it and I knew it. "Get in the truck and stay put till I get back."

"Why can't I come?"

"Just stay here." His face flicked dark and light as the sign next door flashed, *All Topless at Teddy's*.

He marched away from the truck. I watched him get smaller and dimmer through the windshield.

I burst out of the truck and ran.

I followed him down the street, a ways behind him, but he didn't look back. He walked past a bar and I saw through the windows rows of men lined up on stools. One man looked right at me. His face was a dark moon. I hurried past.

The Prince turned at the corner onto Sassafras Lane. He walked by an empty lot. I kept back in the shadows and ran by the tall grass quick and stepped behind a mailbox when he stopped in front of a small square building with just two dice blinking up above the door. First one blinked, then both blinked together.

The Prince went up two steps, then through the door.

I was left behind the mailbox.

I went up to the front door. It was black and padded like a leather car seat with a tiny window up at the top. The building was not tall enough for a big staircase. There were no windows to peek in.

I stood out in front and looked up at the blinking dice. The door started to open, so I ran, rat-quick, to the side of the building where the garbage cans were. There were beer bottles spilling out of them. I heard music playing. It sounded thick and dull like when I wrapped my pillow around my ears to keep from hearing my mom and dad yelling.

I went round back and heard silverware and plates rattling. I heard the sound of water running. The back door was open. I climbed up the back stairs. When I peeked in I saw a little black woman with big arms washing a tub of greasy dishes. She had a hairnet on her head. Her hair was so squashed down by the hairnet it made her head too small for her body. In a minute, she went off through a swinging door with a stack of clean dishes.

Quickly I ran across the kitchen floor, slipsliding in my good black shoes in the grease and water. I went through the swinging door after the woman.

When I got through that door I was standing in a little hallway. Down the hallway I could see a curtain. The swinging doors opened. I pressed back in the dark. When the doors opened I heard music playing loud, people laughing and talking. I heard something break and more laughing and clapping.

I went up to the red velvet curtain and peeked through. I saw a stage like the stage at our school, only bigger, with a part that went out into the audience. The audience was mostly men. I saw the Prince out there in the front.

The way he sat there, with a mug of beer sheltered in his hands, between two other men, he looked to me like the last one to be picked in red rover.

Music started. I could see two people in the band on the other side of the stage. One was a piano player with long grey hair. When he banged the keyboard, crashing chords came out. Another man, who looked like he was maybe Spanish, maybe Italian, played an electric guitar, plum purple. He stroked it slow and picked the strings in long wails and fits.

Clematis walked right by me. I smelled her up.

She smelled of honeysuckle and tobacco. As she walked by me in the shadow of the curtain, she brushed against me but didn't even look, didn't even see. She pushed through a slit in the curtain and stood out there on the stage. I could see by craning my head through that little slit.

It looked as if my momma was the whole show. Men stood up in the audience when she walked out on the stage. I was knocked over by the twinkling of her costume. Her long gown was see-through pink, long like a princess, soft as baby skin. It glittered in the lights the way stars might if you caught them in a net. She had diamonds in her hair, which was twisted into red-gold shimmery curls. On her wrists were more diamonds. She even had a diamond in her belly-button.

She dipped down like a ballet dancer and the audience hooted and yelled. She nodded over to the other side of the stage and the lights went all soft. The music, different now, started playing.

Clematis walked slowly around that little space. She looked taller in that light, blue light that made her skin glow white as marble, made her arms and legs look longer. The light made a shadow that seemed to grow out of her, that raised up over her on the curtain behind her.

Then she started to sing.

> *I had a sweet man—he was as good as gold.*
> *Tell me honey why you act so cold?*
> *Don't my lips make you holler*
> *and cry out for more?*
> *I gotta make a dollar that's for shore.*
> *So come here darlin' and feel some heat.*
> *What baby?*
> *Huh sugar?*
> *Why you act so cold?*

Oooh honey,
Aaah baby,
Why you act so cold?

She sang it once, this song, all soft and fuzzy, her eyes half shut like she was dreaming the song and the song was her dream that she shared with everyone. Then the music got louder and she sang it again, slower, but louder, each word like a bullet to the heart.

When she sang "He was as good as gold," she rubbed her legs, she rubbed her breasts, but not like she was cold—smooth and dreamy.

"I gotta make a dollar"—She took down the straps of her starry gown right over her blue-white shoulders. First one, then the other, very slowly. They flapped there, under her arms while she peeled off her gloves, pure white with little pearls sewn on, and she threw them out into the audience. One man knocked over his drink reaching out to catch it.

"So come here darlin"—She unzipped her dress. She turned away from the audience. I could see her eyes, face turned toward me hiding in the shadows. She wiggled, a fish, a mermaid, out of the dress and it laid there on the stage, nothing now without Clematis.

On her breasts were diamonds. They were pasted to her with tassels hanging down. The tassels made a swinging shadow on her stomach.

"Feel some heat"—She rubbed her hands between her legs. She had on some tiny, sparkly underpants that went right up between the crack in back.

The audience was yelling hoarse and mean.

The shadow danced ten feet high behind her.

She kicked out one foot, the music played slow and cruel. She planted that foot down and kicked the other foot. She walked down the stage into the audi-

ence and did circles with her hips. She turned around
and wiggled her backside at the whiskery man reaching up to touch her.

She moved back, quick but light.

I noticed her eyes were looking above their
heads, as though she didn't really see or hear them at
all.

She wiggled.

I felt hot and sweaty. My head ached. She wiggled some more while the music scorched my face.

Then it was over.

She swooped down and picked up her dress.

Some man threw a beer can on the stage.

"More!" yelled someone else.

I felt my dad's face pulling me, but I didn't want
to look.

When I saw him, his mouth was a broken
twisted-up thing which held back his insides. I felt his
panic, it was like an animal that smells its own blood,
and as Clematis left the stage I was filled up with his
shame. My mother took off her clothes in front of
people she didn't even know. I got that dirty feeling
like when I let Richie Levy look down my underpants
last summer in our fort in the woods.

My dad left when the music started again. I saw
him wobbling between tables. I saw another man
shove him but he kept going on to the black leather
door.

I was watching him so hard that I didn't see
Clematis see me. I heard a moaning sound behind me
and turned around. She was standing mostly naked,
with her diamonds still sparkling in her hair. She was
looking down at me, her mouth moving like a fish
trying to breathe air.

I ran through the kitchen, slipped on the floor,
but kept going and going out that screen door into the
night.

"Isobel!" I heard her calling.

I ran and ran.

It wasn't that my momma was naked. I'd seen her in soap bubbles, I'd laid on the bed while she tried on rustling dresses for me. She was naked in Sin City. If she ever came home the Prince would smack her up against the wall like he did when he caught her kissing Jesse Sherman.

Naked in Sin City.

She'd never come home now.

But her eyes when she saw me were filled up with the same lost-in-the-wilderness look as my dad's.

I sat down under a big tree in front of a closed Kroger grocery store. I held my breath and counted the stars in the Little Dipper and the Big Dipper.

Then I walked back to the truck.

ten

I get turned in

I went back to the truck and waited in the front seat. I curled up and fell asleep finally, but the air was humid—mosquitoes bit my hands and face and woke me with their buzzing in my ears. I opened my eyes. It didn't take me even a minute to realize that I was alone.

The light was fuzzy through a layer of clouds.

Across the street a restaurant window was half filled up with a blinking blue coffee pot. BOTTOMLESS CUP said a big sign next to the coffee pot. Pink letters glowed *Refrigerated Inside.* My dress was scrunched up, my hair was sticking to my face. My feet went *thrum, thrum,* trapped in the Shirley Temple shoes.

I got out of the truck and walked across to the flickering coffee pot.

I pushed open the door and a big man on a stool swung around to look at me. He had on a hat with a bulldog on it. *Mack,* it said. He had a tattoo on his thin ropy forearm, a blue and red rooster.

"Frances, git out here," shouted the man.

I stood there waiting. I was waiting for Frances, whoever that was.

"What're you yelling for," said the big woman who came out through the swinging doors.

Then she saw me. "Holy, Moly," she said.

"Hi," I said.

"It's another lost kid," said the man with the bulldog hat.

"You lost?" asked Frances.

I shook my head. "My dad's lost. I'm not."

"We had another lost kid last week."

"This place is turning into a regular orphanage," said the man in the hat.

"What happened to the other kid?" I asked. I wanted to be conversational. I didn't really care what happened to the other kid at all. I wanted the chocolate doughnut I saw underneath the plastic cake pan.

Frances had Nehi orange hair that went flying up around her little waitress hat. Her hair looked as if it was being sucked up to heaven.

"Nothing happened to him. His mom came down in a fancy car. What kind of car was that?"

"Bentley, 1958," said the hat man. "Now ya see, ya got your Rolls Royce and ya got your—"

"Like I said, some fancy car," said Frances. "Took him howlin' his head off in the back seat. Just like I told you, Ray, that kid probably never had a happy day in his life until the day he ran away and came here. Money don't necessarily bring happiness."

Ran away, I thought. This kid might be a little bit interesting.

"Lawlor kid. They own the franchise on all those Burger Boys from here to Chicago. You know the Lawlors?"

I shook my head no.

"They got a boat up on Lake Michigan, the kid said. Cabin cruiser, sleeps twelve. Your dad rich?"

"Well, now what?" said the hat man before I could answer Frances.

"What are you asking me for? I don't know. You hungry, kid?"

"Don't you think you should try and find her father?"

"Drop dead, Ray," said the woman. "Where'd your father go?"

I shrugged my shoulders. "Can I have some of those doughnuts?"

She got me two of the doughnuts from the tray—chocolate and glazed—and a glass of milk. I guess I wasn't too polite because I just shoved them in my mouth. When I talked I sprayed some crumbs. "My dad went over to the Magic Club and my momma was there and she took off her clothes, then my dad left and didn't come back to the truck. I have to go to the bathroom," I said.

"Back there," said Frances. "I guess we're not talkin' about a reward here then." She looked at Ray and he rolled up his eyes.

I felt much better after I went to the bathroom. I patted a wet paper towel on my face and brushed the crumbs off my face. I couldn't see in the mirror, but looking in the towel dispenser I smoothed down my hair. I knew now that though things might be bad in the long run, for the short haul they'd be all right. Frances was going to help me find my dad.

When I walked back out to the front of the restaurant there were two more men sitting up by Ray and a few more sitting in the booths. Frances was taking a man's order.

"Are you going to help me find my dad?"

"Not now. I'm the only one on. Go on over to the booth in the back and I'll bring you some ice cream. When it gets to be eight o'clock my relief gets here and we'll go on over to the police station. What do you mean your mother took off her clothes at the Magic Club?"

"I don't want to go to the police station," I said.

Frances bent over from the waist so fast I had to duck quick. "Look, kid," she said, and not in too nice a voice. "I'm working. Two choices. Go sit in the booth and I'll take you there personally so you can find your dad, or number two, I'll call them up on that phone there and have them come get you in a squad car."

I considered my two options while the man whose order I'd interrupted glared daggers at me. He was hungry, I guess. I went back to the booth in the corner.

Frances brought me cherry jubilee ice cream. I picked out all the cherries and left the ice cream to melt to soup.

Finally it was time to go. The other waitress was named Clara Rose and she fussed over me some and asked me some questions, but Frances pulled on a sweater and took me by the hand and out the door we went. We walked to the police station, which wasn't too far, a few blocks.

The courthouse was a big building with columns, and Latin words over the door. We didn't have a courthouse in Morseville. We climbed a lot of steps and saw a little sign with an arrow. POLICE it said and pointed down a long hall.

Sunlight came in through huge windows. As we walked by, the dust in the air danced and glistened. I wanted to stand there a minute in the sunlight on the dark green marble floor and just let that light wash over me, but Frances yanked me again.

"How come I gotta go to the police, Frances?"

"'Cause I'm a good citizen," she said.

"But you're turning me in!" I said.

"Turning you in?" She looked at me funny.

The police department was at the back of the building. We went up to a high counter where a policeman was sitting. I could just see his head.

I'd never been to a police station before. I'd seen "Dragnet" and those men never smiled. I was pretty scared they were going to lock me up for not having a dad. I stood behind Frances.

"I brought a lost kid."

The policeman didn't say anything.

"Hey, Bud," said Frances and poked him in the arm.

"What!"

"What a police force we got here. I'm so glad to know that we're paying our taxes so that you can get your beauty rest."

The policeman looked down over his high counter. I think Frances's hair kind of scared him.

"I got a lost kid and I gotta get outta here. I got an appointment at the beauty shop."

"I'm not lost," I said.

"Who're you?" asked the policeman.

He couldn't see me from up where he sat, small and half behind Frances's legs. He got up and leaned over the counter. He crooked his finger to me, in that come-here way.

"My dad's lost, not me," I said.

"Where do you live?" he asked. His mouth was small and when he talked I didn't notice it moving. I wondered if he could do that thing with puppets, you know, throw his voice, like Howdy Doody.

"Rural route three, box two-nineteen, Morse-ville, also called Shady Acres Fine Swine Farm."

"What's your dad's name?"

"Prince Roundtree."

"What's he Prince of?" He laughed.

"Ha, ha," went Frances.

"Hee, ha, ha," went the policeman.

"Look, I gotta get goin'," said Frances. "I done my civic duty." She looked down at me. "Sure your daddy's not rich?"

I shook my head.

"Got a reward that last time. Well," she looked thoughtful for a minute and gave me a smile, "not too much profit in pigs, I guess."

She turned and left without even a goodbye.

"Wait," hollered out the policeman. "I gotta have your name for the file."

But she was gone or not answering.

"Her name is Frances," I told him.

"Frances who?"

I shrugged.

He shrugged back.

"OK, he said. "Looksee here, actually your dad did come in here a few hours ago and wanted to file a missing persons report. He couldn't because it hadn't been twenty-four hours. You run away?"

"My mom did, but that was a long time ago. We came here to find her. Can I sit down?" I asked him. I felt so tired.

"How did you get lost from your father?"

"I didn't."

"OK, then how'd he get lost from you?"

"I don't know. I lost him after he left the Magic Club."

His eyebrows made a triangle above his nose. "The Black Magic Club! What were you doin' there?"

"I snuck in. He doesn't know I did. Can I sit down now?"

"Your dad's coming back, kiddo, in an hour or so to fill out the report. You can stay back in a room we got here. Funny business. Little kid in a strip joint. He's gonna have to answer a few questions."

He picked up his telephone and started to dial. "Uh, here," he said, "take this pencil and some paper. I don't know, draw or somethin'."

I took the pad and pencil.

A woman in a green uniform came and took me to a small room.

There were no windows in the room, only a bright electric light that made spiders crawl in front of your eyes if you looked directly at it. A red Coke machine and four hardwood chairs was all that was in there. The woman didn't give me any money for the Coke machine. She closed the door behind her.

Even though I wasn't a prisoner I felt like one.

I pretended to be one.

I walked the floor and measured it with my feet. Twelve across, fifteen down. No windows, just that bright light. I tried the door. It was locked. I *was* a prisoner.

I sat down on one of the wooden chairs, chairs just like the ones in Mr. Martin's office. These chairs had two little hollows carved out for the rear end to settle in, but I was too small to reap their benefit.

My dad hadn't forgotten me.

I saw my momma in my head. There was nothing else to see in that room. I kept seeing her mouth trying so hard to talk to me and not able to make even the tiniest sound. Even though she was dressed only in diamonds, all I saw was her mouth. That mouth made tears start at the corners of my eyes.

The door of the room swung open and the green-uniformed woman brought in the tallest woman I had ever seen.

Emma Swallow.

That was how I met her.

Emma Swallow—six foot three in stocking feet.

eleven

Sometimes things change but you don't know it

Tall. I watched as the uniformed police lady sat her down in one of the hard chairs and took off a pair of handcuffs. Even sitting in the chair she was so tall the ceiling seemed lower. She hunkered down as if afraid it might press down her shoulders.

The police lady went out the door, closing it behind her. I could hear the handcuffs clinking as she walked away down the hall.

The criminal sat hunched over in her chair, her head in her hands. I could see red lines on her wrists where the handcuffs had rubbed. She had black hair, or maybe it was brown, I couldn't really tell because it was so greasy. I could see her scalp where her hair parted, pink as bologna lunchmeat. She didn't have on any shoes. Her stockings were full of holes and runs that disappeared into her dirty blue housedress.

I crossed my legs at the ankles and swung them back and forth, making a clunking noise every time my shoe heels brushed the floor. She still didn't look up.

Her shoulders were shaking and she rocked to and fro in the chair, her head still locked in the safety of her arms. I thought she was crying. I crouched down at her feet, turned my head sideways, and looked up into a face so full of misery my heart pinched and left me hurting. I jumped back in my chair. She had those beaten-dog eyes.

I wished my dad would come.

I went over and looked in the Coke machine. The bottle caps said, *Coke, 7-Up, NeHi, Coke, Coke, Coke.* I read them all through the glass door. I almost died when I turned around. The woman was sitting with her dress all run into the center of her lap between her duck-planted legs. Her elbows hung down from her shoulders as if they were wired there. Her hands made me think of dirty Play-Doh. She was looking right at me.

I brushed out my dress, kind of shuffled around, twisted my hair around my finger—my worst habit, my momma used to say. Made me look like a moron. I dropped my hands to my sides and sat back down.

A woman criminal, tallest woman criminal ever maybe, was looking me over with those sick, sad eyes.

"Did you murder somebody?" It was all I could think to ask.

She sighed and filled the room with garlicky air.

"I can't get any Cokes because they didn't give me any money." She glanced away from me over to the Coke machine.

"My dad's coming to get me. He's tall as you."

She looked down at her hands and stuck one into her housedress and pulled out a little leather bag that was pinned inside. She fished out two dimes and held them out to me.

I took them.

"Do you want Coke, NeHi, or 7-Up?" I asked her. She shrugged.

"Welp," I said, after trying the 7-Up, "looks like they're out of that one." The dime came clattering back. I tried again and pushed Coke and opened it up for her. Brown fizz rose out of the neck.

She took it from me and just held it.

I got a Coke, too.

"How old are you?" Her voice was almost deep as a man's, but soft.

"Eleven. How old are you?"

"Twenty-nine."

"Oh," I said.

I asked her if she was poor.

She said nothing. She started to cry. I hated the way that she cried. There was no sound, just these great big thick tears that gobbed up around her mouth, then slid down, one by one, and splashed on her Coke bottle. Some actually went right into the neck of the bottle. She would be drinking tears if she ever stopped crying and took a swallow.

She looked up at me.

"What they got you here for?" I asked.

"Vagrancy."

"What's that?"

"They said it's when you don't got no home."

"You haven't got a home?"

"'Course I do! I got family, lots of 'em." She snuffled some tears up her nose.

"What're you doin' here, then?"

"You ask a lot of questions, girl. T'ain't polite."

I hung my head over my Coke bottle.

"Come here," she said.

I looked at her. She smelled bad even from three feet away. She had dirt on her so thick you could've drawn a picture on her face with a thumbnail.

"Come on over here. I don't bite."

She looked like she might, though.

I walked over. I wasn't going to be a chicken liver.

"Give me your right hand. No, your right hand!"

I shuffled hands. She snatched my hand, peered deep at my palm.

She smiled at me. Her top teeth were as crooked as our peeling picket fence. Her eyes didn't have the beaten-dog look anymore. They looked at me sly-like. She looked deep into my face, then back at my palm. I got a shiver up my tailbone.

I asked, "Are you reading my palm? Are you a fortuneteller?"

"Yew got some momma. She's a pretty woman, am I right?"

I nodded my head.

"She's a church-goin' woman."

"Nope," I said.

"Well," said the woman, "she used to be."

"Maybe," said me.

"She's got yeller hair."

"Nope."

"OK, brown then."

I shook my head no.

"It's brown, she dyes it … red!"

"It is red, but she doesn't dye it. At least I don't think so." The criminal held my palm right up under her nose.

"Now, yew got a dog, a big yeller dog named, named, Cricket." She looked at my face. "Now, don't tell me, it's Joe, no Blacky. I got it! It's Punkin!"

I didn't have a dog, but I didn't tell her.

"Yew got a little brother. I see it here." She pulled my palm up to my face and pointed to a crossed line with a broken fingernail. "Your daddy's a gay man, always laughin'."

"I never had a brother."

She threw down my hand and leaned back on her chair. Her face was set, her eyes burning right at me.

"He died in your momma's womb."

"Oh," I said. "I never knew that."

"Humpf," she said.

"What are you doing here, I mean here in Terre Sacre?"

She sipped her Coke and wiped her mouth with her hand. "You're a nosy thing, ain't ya?"

"Well, what are you doing here in a jail? You must of done something wrong."

She stood. I looked up. Sitting in my chair I was directly in front of a red dahlia on the crotch of her housedress.

"The curious foxy lost his tail in the henhouse."

"It's the curious cat lost his tail in the door."

She glared at me. "Where I come from it's a foxy and a henhouse." She turned away.

"Look," I said to her skinny backbone, "I'm sorry I was nosy. I just wondered why you were sad was all."

"I'll tell you somethin'." She sat back down and leaned across to me from her chair. "I've got a good mind to turn that police gal into a big brown toad."

"Are you a witch, too?" My mind was reeling.

She winked a silvery eye at me. "Don't you pay no nevermind. I got ways to deal with these here folks."

She smiled again. I thought I saw for a second in those silver eyes a fire burning, flames shooting tall. Then it was gone.

She slumped back in her chair with her mouth open wide. She seemed to collapse into herself to make herself small.

"What are they gonna do with you?"

"Don't know." She smiled. "Maybe I'll burn this place down around their ears."

The fire in her eyes! I grinned my little monkey grin. "My dad is coming here soon."

She wasn't looking at me anymore. She was looking at the lines on her own right palm.

"Hey, we live ... do you have a pencil?" She

didn't answer me. I remembered the pad and pencil the policeman had given me. I'd put it under my chair. I printed our address as neat as I could. "Look here."

But she didn't.

"Look, this is my address." I held out the paper and it fluttered into her lap. "My dad will help you if you don't have a home. My mom ran away."

She looked up. "Ran away? I didn't see that."

The door opened up and I ran to it expecting my dad, but it was only the green-uniformed police lady. "Come with me, young lady," she said.

"Remember," I told her.

Last I saw she was turned away from me, her hands up to block away the light.

The police lady closed the door with a bang.

"That woman is a pain in the neck. Did she bother you?"

I said no.

"I can't believe he stuck her in there with you."

"She wouldn't hardly talk to me."

"Well, that's what you really call your white trash. Stinks like a monkey in the zoo."

I looked up at the woman who was holding my hand. I pulled my hand away. I didn't want to be holding hands with a big warty old toad. "What's her name?" I asked, all angel-innocent.

"Swallow somethin'—Emma, I think. Who cares? Good riddance to bad rubbish!"

I heard someone calling me and I forgot for the moment about Emma Swallow.

My dad had come to get me.

twelve

Mr. Potter visits and I talk to trees

Summer had waded in. It was hot. On Sunday mornings I'd lay on my stomach over the pages of the funny papers. Prince Valiant and Dick Tracy ran right off the page in a blur of color as my sweat rolled off my face and hit the paper.

I hadn't seen Richie Levy at all. He hadn't come racing down our gravel driveway on his bike, skidding at the end, or waited for me by our fort in the woods. I figured he must have been sent to his grandma's out in California, but I couldn't figure out why he hadn't come and said goodbye.

One morning I had gone over to his house and knocked on his back door. I hardly ever went over there. He preferred to come play at my house because nobody at my house cared what we did. His mom was always poking her nose in while we played in his room. I knocked on his back door.

Richie's mom opened the door, only partly. I could see their shiny kitchen floor, bright black and pink squares. I looked at her eyeglasses. The glass part was dark green. They had thick black frames. She had weak eyes, Richie had told me. Light hurt her.

"Can Richie come out?" I asked her glasses. I never saw her eyes. Sometimes I suspected she didn't have any at all; just holes behind the glasses. She relied on those other eyes—the ones in the back of her head.

"Richie is in California." She was going to close the door right in my face.

"He's not home?"

"Listen," she opened the door just a little bit more, "Richie isn't going to play with you anymore."

"How come?"

"Because."

"Because why?" I smiled my angel best.

"What?" she said. She paused for a moment and looked at me. "That has nothing to do with it."

"What doesn't?"

"About your mother."

"I didn't say anything about my mother."

I stood there for a moment more—long enough for Mrs. Levy to shut the door in my face.

"Richie's a retardo anyway," I said to the door.

I stomped off to our yard.

So as far as summer was concerned, it wasn't the same and not just because Richie couldn't play with me or because my momma still didn't come home.

Clematis sent me a card from Chicago, Illinois, with Lassie on it. "Come home," the dog barked in the cloud over its head. "I miss you."

How dumb—that was just like Clematis—I *was* home. She was the one who wasn't.

Summer didn't even smell like summer or maybe I smelled it differently that year. Nobody took care of the vegetable garden so it got tangled up with pumpkin vines and the tomatoes ran wild and rotted. Every time I walked back by the garden I'd dart in and squash a few. They exploded with tomato blood. It splashed on my legs and ran down in streaks, dried, then crusted.

I smelled different that summer. Fear puts a different odor on you.

Now Mr. Potter was in the living room. Mr. Potter with his big silver car was sipping a beer with my dad and talking to him about the big money he could make. We could be rich if he sold the land. It was a different Mr. Potter than the one who taught Sunday school at First Church of God the Redeemer.

"Yeah," I heard him say through the screen window on the porch, "just thirty-some acres of that property back there could get you a nice fifteen, twenty thou."

I could hear my dad shifting around on the creaky couch. Then he spied me at the window.

"Get away from that window—my daughter," he said to Mr. Potter, who laughed. I stood there shooting the evil eye at Mr. Potter. "Go on now," said my dad.

I pretended to leave. I clumped down the porch stairs then snuck back up by the window.

"Yes, well you know, Roundtree, I built that housing development next to you and I'd like to see Cornwall Commons expanded. The need's growing, you know. We're gonna explode here, and people have gotta live somewhere. Why, you might think I'm crazy now, but I think people'll even commute from here to Louisville."

"Why the hell would they wanna do that?" asked my dad. "Why'd anybody wanna drive thirty miles to a job and back every day?"

"You got it all here. You got your beautiful nature, you got your low housin' costs, and you got your commutability."

Can someone have a greasy voice? Because he did. Mr. Potter's voice usually sounded soft and fat or full. He was fat. His voice matched him. But now his voice sounded dipped in hot lard.

"Hell," said my dad again, "you want me to sell off thirty acres of God-given beauty so that you can build cardboard houses like they got next door?"

Yeah, I thought to myself. Go, Daddy.

"Roundtree," said Mr. Potter, "do you honestly want to sell hogs for the rest of your life? You must have a dream, you must want something better. Here you are, man on his own, growing girl—what are you gonna do? Bacon pay for college?"

I heard my dad shift around in the chair. I heard him thinking.

"Can you say you couldn't use twenty-five, thirty thousand dollars?"

"Thirty thousand," whispered my dad.

"Or more," said Mr. Potter.

"More?" asked my dad.

"Beautiful houses for everyone to live in. Neat, clean, little green patches of heaven! But I know," his voice dropped down, got soft, got wiggly as a snake, "that heaven has a price and we all got to pay the price. I'll pay that price, Roundtree, I'll pay that price."

Punch him, I thought, punch him good.

Just then I slipped on the tilted board underneath the window. *Bang* I went as my head hit the screen. The screen quivered.

"Issy, you get away from that window now!" shouted my dad.

I did, but not before I heard him telling Mr. Potter he would think about it.

I went out to the woods and sat among the hanging vines by the mound that I was sure was an Indian grave. Sitting by the dead Indian, I knew everyone was going to die but me.

It'd start with Clematis. Instead of a birthday card in August I'd get one of those telegram things. Dead in the War. I wasn't sure which war. If there wasn't one in the place she was in, Clematis'd start her own. My momma. I picked up a stick and stabbed a beetle. I felt bad when I saw he was still alive. His legs moved crazy, each one a different way. I took pity and smashed him.

Then the Prince. He'd die of grief and drinking Pabst Blue Ribbon beer. He didn't care a lick about me anymore, anyway. He cared more about his hogs.

Grandma and Grandpa Roundtree were already dead. They were rotting up at the church cemetery just like the mole I buried. I dug it up after three months had passed to see what had happened. Pieces of skin hung off it like too-loose clothing. I could see the tiny white bones and its little sharp teeth. I buried it up nice again—it looked so naked without its fur.

Out in the woods I talked to the trees. It was the only way I could calm down, be peaceful. I sang to the trees. Talking to the trees gave me a kind of deep-down power. I could feel it running into me where I touched their tough bark. I would lean up against them and smell the sap deep inside—tree blood.

My grandpa, who died when his heart exploded while he was shoveling snow, never had the trees cut down to plant more land. My grandpa knew about trees.

I remember my Grandpa Roundtree very clearly showing me the worms—how they come out after the rain and lay all over the ground like spaghetti. I cried when I saw the birds eat up all those helpless worms. Here they'd crawled out of the earth to keep from drowning and now they were being eaten up for their trouble.

How did my grandpa know why I was crying? But he did. I remember he squeezed my hand. "They're part of the Lord's blessing for the growing world, Issy. They feel no pain."

He keeled over not too long after that.

I'd really like to have known my grandpa better, I thought, while I sat in the woods with the sunlight breaking up in shadows on the mossy ground.

It got later and later. I didn't go home for dinner.

That night, leaning against a tree, getting hungry, I thought about sneaking back to the house to get some saltines or something, but I was determined to stay gone all night.

I wasn't really sure my dad would notice.

We had a bit of moon that night in the woods. I never stayed in the woods past twilight before. I sat there slapping mosquitoes and remembering my dad saying, "More?" What's more?

I kissed the tree I leaned against. Yes, I kissed it like a sister and then I went back to the house.

As I walked past the mirror at the bottom of the stairs, I got caught and in I fell just like into a pool of moonlit water.

In the mirror all alone I looked for my mother. I found her looking for me—her eyes, her lips, and the scoop of her neck where it hollowed out by the bones. Then my momma and I were dancing in the mirror, arms about each other and arms growing from four to two.

We didn't see my dad standing in the doorway, standing just outside the mirror. I whispered to momma that daddy would sell the woods if she didn't come home to keep him quiet. She laughed, her teeth bone-white and perfect.

"He needs you, Momma." We swung around and around until my dizziness made stars.

"Knock it off," I heard my daddy's voice, all soft. I heard him even inside the mirror, and Momma turned her face to him.

"Prince," she said and she used my lips. "Dance with me, Prince." My momma's eyes trapped his and held them to her, not letting them go.

I didn't see him coming. I didn't see his hand. My momma ran off deep into the mirror, singing, laughing.

He punched me clean in the eye.

Later, deep at night he brought me ice cubes in a washrag and held it to my eye. I heard him crying, but I pretended to sleep.

I dreamed of trees.

thirteen

Sunflower love

I was running the Hoover vacuum over the rug in the sitting room when I thought I heard knocking at the door. I peeked around the foofey drapes that Clematis had hung, but I didn't see anyone.

I turned on the vacuum again and finished up the rug. I was bending down to unplug the cord when I heard this tapping on the window glass. I stood up and saw a dress with what looked to be swans swimming across it and looked up more and more and saw Emma Swallow.

She stood there, outside the window in her bird-printed dress, with her hands folded as neat as you please in front of her.

I ran outside, slamming the screen door.

"Yes," she said, "I came."

"Well, sit down. Be careful, these rockers catch your hair." I saw that she had a brown grocery sack with her that seemed full of clothes. "Are you going to live with us?" I asked.

"It depends. It depends on the needs of you and your folks."

"My mom is still run off and my dad's, well, my dad's not himself lately, but we need you, I'm sure. Emma Swallow," I said, "they said at the jail that you're white trash. I don't believe them. For instance, you look different now. You're clean and your dress is very pretty."

"Thank you," she said.

"Did you break out of jail?"

"Lord, no." She laughed. When she laughed her mouth opened up and I saw those picket fence teeth. Her eyes were blue with bits of silver running in them like a river. "The chief of police gave me a job as a housekeeper. I saved exactly fifty-two dollars of the money he paid me. My bus fare was six-fifty to git here so I figure I ain't gonna be gittin' too far on what's left."

"So, do you need a home?" I asked. I kept up a conversation because I was afraid she might not like it at our farm. Not too many people can tolerate pigs, and the house paint was peeling. "We have a big console television," I said.

I liked her. I liked her teeth. I liked her melting-ice eyes. I liked her on my front porch, gliding on the rockers. She brought with her, besides the sack of clothes, a feeling a sureness. It was like she knew where she was going. Also, I felt I could've sat on her knee right then and she wouldn't have shoved me off.

"I'm thinkin' in the way of bein' your house-keeper. I don't eat much. And your daddy wouldn't have to pay me too much either."

"Oh, I'm sure he'll like it, Emma Swallow," I said. "He'll like somebody to cook and stuff. I can't, and all he can make are hamburgers and pork ribs."

She looked at me close, then looked away. I thought she'd start crying again. "Well, we'll see."

Emma Swallow was sitting on the glider next to me. I put out my hand and patted her knee. She touched my hand back quicklike, felt like a moth had landed briefly on the back of my hand.

"You must miss your mother."

"I do. But then again, I don't."

"Surely you love your mother, honey."

"Yes," I said. "I love her, but she's not too reliable. She's a singer, you know, and professional. She's a bad mom and a bad wife, but I'm proud of her.

Someday I want to be a singer, too." I didn't really, but nobody ever had anything nice to say about Clematis. The Prince wouldn't even say her name since he came back from Terre Sacre.

"My dad's laying down in the back room," I told her. "My dad gets these headaches lately. His head aches so bad it almost makes him blind."

"Sound's to me like megraine."

"What's that?"

"It's a headache that makes you want to die. My brother used to get them. What you need is quiet and broth and a room where the winders are blacked out. Take me to the kitchen."

I showed Emma Swallow the kitchen and before I could say boo, she was making a chicken stock from the hen in the refrigerator, adding basil from the plant by the back stoop and fresh pepper and garlic and onion. From the little bag pinned inside her dress she sprinkled some black powder into the pot.

"What's that?" I asked as I leaned over the stove.

"That, child, is the ground-up big toe of a twice-born man."

"Yech," I said. "What for?"

"Keeps the devil from settlin' in the brow. He likes it there, close to the brain. When the head is weakened by one of these here megraines, the devil gits his chance to worm his way in."

"My daddy don't believe in the devil."

"Well, he should. Old Black Toes don't care whether you do or not though," said Emma Swallow.

"How can a man be twice born?"

"Born onct of his momma and onct of the Lord." Emma Swallow dipped down into the stock with a ladle and let me have a taste. I tasted summer air in the herbs.

"The secret to a good stock is letting it sit for a day or two, but we don't have time." I shook my head, agreeing with her. "Also, fresh-killed chicken is best—this old?"

"Pretty old, week or so."

"We'll do what we can. Go cut me a sunflower out by that fence there."

"A sunflower?"

She didn't answer, so I went and brought back one of the big flowers, a flower as big as a plate.

"Now, what's your name?" It just hadn't occurred to me that I never told her my name.

"It's Roundree," said Emma. "Know that from the mailbox out by the road, but what's your given name?"

"Isobel," I said. "I'm named after my mother's dead sister."

"Isobel, you scoop out that middle there of that sunflower with a spoon."

"How come?"

"We'll make a special bowl to eat broth from and sunflowers have got special properties, powers to heal and soothe everything from the heart to the liver."

"What about heads?"

"I'm not sure, but it'll look nice. That's good, Isobel."

I looked at the sunflower bowl. It wouldn't hold much, but it did look cheerful and certainly different. I wondered if my dad would eat out of a flower, though. I suspected he'd think it was awfully strange.

When the broth was ready, Emma spooned it into the bowl and we put it on a tray and covered it with a clean, white, cotton dish towel. On a separate plate, Emma put some saltine crackers with just a bit of oleo.

I carried the tray. Emma followed me to my dad's room.

I walked in first. The Prince was laying on his back, flat and still, his eyes closed.

"Daddy," I whispered. "I brought you some soup."

"Put it down, punkin. I'll eat it later." He didn't open his eyes.

"You should eat it now, Mr. Roundtree."

My dad sat up halfway in bed. His face was white and there was sweat running down from his forehead.

"Who're you?"

"I'm Emma Swallow, Mr. Roundtree. Your little gal and me knows each other from awhile back. I made you a healin' broth." The Prince lay back down. "Plump those pillows, Isobel."

I did. Daddy groaned when he had to lift his head.

"Put that piller right underneath his neck now, not like that." Emma Swallow took the pillow out of my hand and rolled it up. She lifted up the Prince's head gentle and placed it right under his neck. "Now, when you're feeling better we'll talk, Mr. Roundtree. That broth has got a powerful charm in't. Eat it all."

"Charm?" said the Prince with his eyes half open.

"Now, then, Isobel here'll feed ya, there you go, and I've got to start on supper for her. If you need anything else, just holler."

Emma Swallow's head almost hit the frame as she went out the doorway.

"That's the tallest woman I've ever seen."

"I know," I told my dad. "She's gonna be our housekeeper. I know her from before."

But my dad had laid back down, the tray with the sunflower resting there on his chest. He had fallen asleep and I thought his face looked to have just a bit more color.

From the kitchen I heard the clatter of pots and pans being shifted around—Emma Swallow was looking for something—and I just hugged myself and grinned.

I caught myself grinning in my dad's mirror, a picture I took in my head for later. In the background of the reflection in the mirror I saw my dad lying there with his eyes closed, the big sunflower yellow and brown on his chest.

Emma Swallow. Was she from the moon or deepest Kentucky? I ran to the sound of dinner being made.

Later on I went back in to check on the Prince. The sunflower was still on the tray, the tray was next to him on the bed. All the broth was gone.

I smoothed his hair back from his forehead, it'd gotten long.

My daddy.

fourteen

The Prince warms up

At first the Prince skirted around Emma. If she was in the kitchen, my dad went out on the porch. If she followed him out there to ask him, say, what he wanted for dinner, he shoved his hands in his pockets and muttered, "Anything's fine," and then took off for the barn to check on his hogs. I wondered what he was afraid of, exactly.

Once Emma took over, the house was clean and our old beat-up furniture smelled of lemon oil. In July she started canning preserves. We had gooseberries growing wild along our back fence. She made little tiny pies out of them. She'd staked up the tomatoes and brought along the squash and watermelon.

I'd see her out there in the early morning sometimes, doing something with a stick that she used to make little drawings with on the ground. Once when I couldn't sleep, I looked out my window and saw her drawing a line with that stick all around the garden late at night in the moonlight.

We never had such big tomatoes.

My dad had put in about forty acres of soybeans to the east of the house. Out the window of the kitchen I'd see him walking down the rows, bending down to look at the plants—rubbing a leaf clean with a finger. Sometimes I saw him just sitting out there like an Indian chief, smoking one of his Camel cigarettes. Mostly he stayed away from us. Somehow without talking about it that I know of, he and Emma had come to some kind of agreement. She didn't nose around in his business and I figure he was relieved to not have to eat pork ribs or hamburgers every night.

Emma Swallow became a part of our lives like she'd been there all along. My dad didn't have another headache after she came. But he seemed skittish as a rabbit around her all the same. He hardly ever talked to me.

The Prince had taken to buying a whole case of Pabst Blue Ribbon every day or two. During the week he'd either sit in front of the TV watching anything that was on or go out to the barn and drink beer with his hogs. He poured Elmo, the black hog he raised from a shoat, beer in a bowl and they both guzzled till late at night.

I really did believe he loved Elmo more than me. Elmo was crossed with an Arkansas razorback—about the meanest hog on the face of the earth. Elmo just adored my daddy. He'd rub up against him, all six hundred-odd pounds of him, rub right up against the Prince's legs like a cat.

The Prince would talk to him.

I spied on them. It got to be real work sometimes. I was afraid for the Prince to catch me. I didn't know exactly what he might do.

"Hell, Elmo," he said one time while I peeked through the hole in the barnwood, "women is the last thing on my mind." Like Elmo had asked my daddy a question and he was answering him. "You got it made, boy," said the Prince. "Get 'em in the springtime and then good riddance."

On Saturday nights the Prince would take the truck and go off somewhere. He never said where and we didn't ask. I'd hear the gears slipping and spinning and the radio turned up real loud to some country station, fiddle music mostly. He'd back out the driveway and roar away down the road. I'd just see black smoke left in the air when I got to the end of the drive.

I couldn't sleep until the Prince got home, usually late at night. I'd hear his boots on the wooden porch stairs and the screen door slam behind him, then heavy steps as he went down the hallway to his bedroom.

The rhythm of his boots on the linoleum made me wonder if he was dancing some kind of strange two-step. I'd hear a hollow boom down there sometimes like he'd run right into the wall.

One Saturday night after he'd cleaned up his plate, sopped up all the gravy with Emma's homemade biscuits, he turned on the radio in the kitchen. He lit up a cigarette and sat back down to the table.

I looked at Emma and she looked at me.

"Well, Isobel, git that rhubarb pie off the back stoop if the cats ain't gotten to it already."

I brought in the pie. It was still warm and pinked the palms of my hands. Emma sliced a piece for each of us.

The Prince smoked his cigarette. "That was Miss Patsy Cline and 'I Fall to Pieces' on KNCR, the *only* country station."

My dad tapped the top of the radio. "You think I don't know you listen to that radio up in your room?"

"What, daddy?" I asked.

"Bring me a beer there, punkin." I raced to the refrigerator and reached in back to find the coldest one.

"Miss Swallow," said the Prince, "would you care for a beer?"

I looked at Emma and she nodded to me. "I surely wouldn't mind one in this heat."

I opened the beers and gave them each a plastic glass. "Can I have a drink of yours, Daddy?" I asked.

He let me take a sip out of that brown bottle. The beer tingled in my nose and tasted salty. I didn't like it.

"Um, that's good," I said. "Can I have some more?"

"Eat your pie, Issy," said my dad and I did.

We all sat there, the sun down, the crickets chirping. From a house over in Cornwall Commons we could hear the thin sound of a TV game show. My dad got out his nail clippers and started clipping his fingernails.

My dad turned up the radio when a fiddle man started the slow choo choo of the Orange Blossom Special.

"When I was a little boy," said the Prince, "my dad took me to the Kentucky State Fair. This place is nothing now, this farm, because I'm a lazy man."

"Oh, now, you're not at all," said Emma Swallow.

"Miss Swallow, I'm a good-for-nothin' when it comes right down to it. My dad knew about farming and work. I know hogs. Fact is, I'm probably gonna have to, well, never mind that now. Anyhow, I'm not a farmer. A farmer does more than raise hogs."

The song was picking up steam as the Orange Blossom Special took off down the tracks. The fiddle rounded curves, went through tunnels, and wove its way clean through the country and went on racing to some happy place.

"This fair was the biggest I'd ever seen. Issy, you never saw anything like this fair here in Clermont County. We're not talkin' old ladies making pies and jam and a few ragtag cows and pigs, we're talking a State Fair." He brushed his clipped nails into a neat pile in the center of the table.

"Was there a Ferris wheel and a haunted house?"

"There was the biggest Ferris wheel I ever saw and my dad took me up to the very top and then, I was surprised because—"

"Because it stopped at the very top!" I said.

"Just like you did with me!" I remembered sitting in that seat, rocking back and forth at the top of the Ferris wheel. The Prince and me sat up there for what seemed like an hour and looked at the lights and tried to pick Clematis out of the crowd.

"Right. There wasn't a haunted house, there was better than that. They had wild animals from Africa with two heads, they had women horseback riders from Arabia. I thought they had everything you could ever want. That night had a rodeo with riders from Texas, professionals. I'd never seen anything like it. You know what a Brahma bull is, punkin?"

I said I didn't.

"It's a huge bull with a big hump, like a camel almost, and the cowboys ride them. Oh, you should have seen it. But, what I'm getting to is, and what this song make me think of ..."

He stopped to drink some beer and light a cigarette.

"I hope I'm not boring you, Miss Swallow."

"Oh, land, no." Emma Swallow pulled her hair back out of her face and positively beamed those witch eyes at my daddy.

"Well, we went into this big tent after the rodeo, just me and my dad. They had the lights all rigged up so that the place was as bright as day. There was a big stage up to the front.

"My dad shoved us through so that we could stand right at the front at the edge of the stage. Across the back wall was a big banner that read, Kentucky State Fiddle Contest.

"A man came up to the big microphone and announced that the first round would be the eight to fifteen year olds. I think I was about eight or nine then myself. This little boy came out with a fiddle and a bow. Now these things were homemade, you understand. These fiddles weren't bought in a music store. It was the prettiest little fiddle. This boy puts the fiddle under his chin and oh, Lord, I thought real birds were singing. This child wasn't any older than me and he made that fiddle speak a language all its own.

"Most of the children were very good, but the first boy was the best and he won.

"The man came back out to the microphone. The next heat, he said, was an open competition—open to all native Kentuckians. So we heard a lot of playing. Lots of people thought they could play and couldn't. Many more played great and had the audience clapping and dancing along.

"Finally, the last entry came out.

"This man was so old I thought he might die before he even got as far as the microphone. He didn't have any shoes and you see, I hadn't really seen too many hillbillies and he was the real thing.

"Then, my dad nudged me, 'This old coot is going to make 'em all crawl back home.' I didn't know what he meant. I was a little bit worried that the man might keel over, and since we were right in front, he might keel over right on us. This man had a beard, white as Santa Claus and longer. Came down to his belt buckle. He put his fiddle at his chest, not under his chin, and started to play real slow and soft.

"Now, some people near to us started to move off, to leave the tent. The old man bowed across the strings and the sounds that came out were chirping crickets, singing doves, and redbirds. You could hear each individual bird call. Listen, I'm telling you he played creation itself. The song he played was basically the beginning of the world and worked itself through to the end. His fingers plucked the strings, between bowing so fast it was a blur.

"I felt my soul lifting off to heaven as he played. The audience was quiet through the whole thing. At the end they went wild and threw hats up in the air.

"He won.

"His name was John McGregor. I'll always re-member that. He won a blue ribbon he didn't thank anyone for. He just shuffled off the stage.

"And that's how I leaned about real fiddle music. Those people played what they heard around them, corn growing and birds singing and the wind in the trees. They couldn't read music and they wouldn't have wanted to. No longhair musician could've touched 'em. They're just about gone now."

We sat quiet. The Orange Blossom Special was getting where it was going, getting fainter and fainter.

The TV across the way blared the theme to "Truth or Consequences."

"I better go out and check the hogs," said my dad.

"I'll clean this up," said Emma Swallow. "I ap-preciated hearin' your story."

Emma Swallow smiled and my dad smiled back. I hadn't seen my dad smile like that in a long time. Then he went out the screen door.

I looked back at Emma and her eyes were all shiny. "Emma, why are you crying?" I asked. Now she was sitting there at the kitchen table and tears were splashing off her wrist.

"Never you mind, girl. I ain't cryin'." She brushed the bits of fingernails off the table and into her lap.

"You homesick for your family?" I asked.

"Those hillbillies? No, siree," said Emma. She unpinned the leather bag from the inside of her dress.

I picked up the pie dishes and put them in the sink.

Emma dropped the fingernail clippings into her little leather bag, pulled the bag closed with the string at the neck. She got up and bumped me away from the sink with her hip. "Go on now," she said.

"Go where?"

"I don't know, find somethin' to do. Land girl, can't you keep yourself busy?" Emma scrubbed at the yellow daisies on the plates. I thought she was gonna scrub them clean off.

I looked up at her face and her eyes had flashes of light in them. I noticed that she had really pretty light brown hair. She had on that dress with the swans again. She always wore that dress or the other one with roses on it when my dad was around.

"What'd you take those fingernails for?" I asked.

"What are you talkin' about, child?" said Emma Swallow. "Git now, I'm busy."

I went out the back door, but my dad had already gone in the barn. He'd left one of his cigarettes lying in the dirt. It was still smoking.

I picked it up and took a big drag off it, pinching the end like I'd seen him do. I felt like I'd inhaled a burning log and choked, but I hung on and took another drag and then another without choking and thought about how my dad had perked up for the first time.

I decided Emma Swallow could like my dad almost as much as me.

fifteen

He comes back

I walked for awhile. I didn't follow the Prince to the barn—I walked out to the soybean field. I followed the humps of dirt, careful not to step on the plants.

It got darker. The house shone with six squares of light.

The sky was purple over the two silos behind the barn. Bats swooped down around me. I'd catch a flash—a quick dark shadow—and then it was gone. When I looked up in the sky I could see the bats darting and twisting, catching insects in the air.

The woods ringing the soybean field looked thick with shadows. I could hear the rustling of branches as night things hunted.

I turned to go back to the house, toward the light and the figure I could see through the kitchen window—Emma washing up the supper things.

With my back to the woods I felt a hand clamp down on my shoulder. It whirled me around in a circle. Around and around I twirled like a girl in a crazy dance. I fell down dizzy on the earth, mashing beans. I smelled night earth, smelled the heat left in it from the sun. When I looked up at the dim figure smiling down at me I knew I was dead.

"Boo!" he said.

All alone in a bean field.

"Hello, little lady, didn't I say I'd be back?" He laughed.

"Hey, Matilda, you're awful quiet tonight. Remember how you talked a blue streak that last time we met?"

I raised myself up off the ground. Looking at him, I backed up slow, my hands flung up, ready to push him back. My heart was ready to crack through my rib cage.

He reached out a hand and pulled me to him by the back of my neck. He had me and he was drawing me to him.

The Cat Man.

And he held me there, a trapped bird in the hand. He tipped my face up but I didn't have to see him to know that his eyes would glow in the dark; two pale green globes of light. They didn't really glow, but glittered in that half light between dusk and final fall of night.

As he looked me over—to kill, I thought, to cook, maybe; that's how his eyes swallowed me up, like choice morsels of meat—I remembered his name. Johnnie Pearl. It wouldn't have sounded like a bad name if I'd of heard it somewhere before I ever saw him.

"Wanna see something?" his voice creamy and sly.

I moved my head left and right as much as I could with his hand clamped to the back of my neck.

"Sure you do, Matilda, all little girls like to see this."

His other hand glided in the air above my nose. I watched his palm as he held it out to me, the inner skin was pale in the air.

"Watch close," he whispered right next to my ear. I felt his warm breath lift the hairs on my neck.

I shut my eyes, but he saw me and shook them open.

"Watch," he hissed.

His hand snaked through the air and I felt a soft

rush of wind behind my ear that made me tremble. His hand went behind his back and I saw something silver—a knife to cut me open shivered in his hand. He placed the cold metal on my nose with my head tilted back and my throat open to the world.

"Put your hand up to your nose, Matilda."

I stood there. I wanted nothing to do with my own death. I'd die like a trapped rabbit.

"Go on." He placed my hand on my nose and felt something hard and round and bigger than a quarter.

"Silver dollar, lucky dollar."

His voice was smiling.

I looked at the silver dollar in the palm of my hand, felt the raised numbers, words, and face.

"Keep it twenty years and it'll be worth somethin'," said the Cat Man.

I wasn't at all sure it wasn't some awful trick. Maybe it would turn into a snake inside my pocket and bite me deep in the leg.

His hand came off the back of my neck. With the coin getting warm from the sweat off my hand, I asked him what he was doing in our soybeans.

"Thinkin' kiddo, thinkin'," he said.

"Why you gotta think so close to our house?" I squeaked—I know I did, but I wasn't gonna run.

"I'm trying to figure something out and I was in the neighborhood."

He sat down in the bean field.

"Hey!" I said. "You're squashin' the beans!"

"Hell, Matilda, a few squashed beans ain't nothin' to worry over. You sit down, too."

I stood there looking down at him.

"Sit down," he said soft and tired. "Please. I gotta ask you something."

I sat down a few feet away from him. I looked him over out of the corner of my eye. His hair had leaves in it. He smelled bad.

"What?"

"Where's your momma?" asked the Cat Man.

"Don't know," I said.

He leaned over and pulled me closer to him by my arm. He smelled of cold sweat and dirty clothes.

"You do know. I've been lookin' and lookin' and I can't find her." He looked me in the eyes. "Where is she?"

He had these real long eyelashes, pretty as a baby girl's. He smiled at me. His big teeth shone bluish in the moonlight. His eyes didn't look right—wild, like an animal's.

"She run off!" I screamed at his face. "So there! I don't know where she is."

He looked up at the moon. I thought he was gonna howl. He said to me, "I'm asking you again, Matilda. I'm being reasonable. I can be a very reasonable man. Think."

The Lassie card two weeks ago had had a photo in it—Clematis in a long dress singing in front of a microphone.

"Last I heard she was singing at a Holiday Inn in Joliet, Illinois." I glared at him.

"When's she coming back, Matilda?"

"I don't know."

He shook me by the arm till my head rattled.

"When," he said, quiet again.

"I don't know," I said. "You're hurting my arm."

"When?"

"Probably never," I said. "She's probably gonna die."

He dropped my arm.

"Not yet, she ain't," said the Cat Man. It seemed like he was talking to himself.

He sat there then, staring at the windows of the house. He looked like a little kid sitting like that, his shoulders slumped down. He pulled his knees up to his chin and rested his face on his dirty blue jeans.

"You stink," I told him. Mixed in with the leaves in his hair were twigs. I saw that now.

"You been sleeping in our woods?" I asked.

He didn't look at me.

"You been sleeping out here in our woods? What do you think you are?"

He looked out across the field. I heard him give a great big sigh.

"What you want my momma for anyway?"

"She is," he looked out toward the house, toward the lights coming from the windows, "my own true love."

"What do you mean?" I asked.

He crumbled up a dirt clod in his hand. The dirt fell through his fingers. "My love is like a red, red, goddamned rose. She still got that hair full of fire?"

"My momma don't know you," I said.

The Cat Man looked at me. "I been away awhile," he said. "I been away a long, long while somewhere dark where they lock you up and throw away the key."

"Prison," I said.

"More like prison than the place itself," sighed the Cat Man.

The moon was stretching the shadows of the trees ringing the field. The house in the distance looked smaller, made me think of a picture postcard.

He tipped my face up in the moonlight.

"You look like her. Not the hair, no, but the eyes and mouth. How could you not have got red hair?" He smiled at me and then he smoothed the hair back from my face very gentle. He tipped my face up to the moon.

"I look like my dad," I said.

The Cat Man laughed a funny, high laugh. "You

do, do you? How is your dad, Matilda? Give him my regards."

"He's fine," I said. "I gotta get going."

I turned away from him and started walking back to the house. I turned back, but he was gone. I heard him crunching twigs in the woods.

"Stop calling me Matilda," I said under my breath. From the woods an owl hooted back at me.

I heard him start to whistle. He whistled and everything else was quiet. I'd heard a whippoorwill a minute ago, but it stopped to listen to this new bird's call. Low and sweet that sound was. Sad as a rainy day. I knew he was in the woods watching me.

I ran for the house.

I didn't tell the Prince that Johnnie Pearl was living in our woods.

sixteen

What's going on

I started hearing noises late at night. Not the regular night noises—creaking in the walls, katydids, cat fights right under my window. Different noises.

I knew Emma was going down the stairs after midnight every night. I'd hear her trying to miss the creaks on the staircase.

I'd fall back to sleep soon after hearing her get to the bottom of the stairs. I was sure she was doing some kind of moon dance out there by the garden.

One night I heard her breathing outside my door, listening, I think, to see if I was asleep. She peeked her head in. I closed my eyes and turned over like I was having a dream. While I was lying there, faking sleep, I suddenly remembered her scraping up the Prince's fingernails and putting them in her little bag.

She tiptoed away from my door and went down the stairs. She must have thought I was sleeping because she didn't even try to step around the creaks on the stairs.

I wondered if my daddy's fingernails had anything to do with what it was she did out there in the moonlight. I decided to follow her.

I got around the squeaks on the floor and stairs better than she did. I'd had more practice. I stopped at the bottom of the stairs for a minute and just listened. I could hear the Prince in his bedroom, sounded like he was talking in his sleep.

My nightgown used to belong to Clematis—what she called a babydoll. The Prince used to say to her when she had it on, "My babydoll in her babydoll. Come and sit on my lap." I'd leave the room when he'd do that. It was palest green and thin, too, so the night air could get in through the material and leave you as cool as if you had nothing on at all.

I shivered.

I went over to the kitchen window and peeked out. I didn't see Emma out there by the garden, not out by the barn either.

I was going to go out the back door onto the stoop when I heard her voice. I didn't hear what she said.

The voice was in my daddy's bedroom.

I leaned against the wall.

I heard her then, plain as day. "Prince," she said. "Oh, come here."

I moved down the hall and stood by the door. It was open a crack. Inside I saw Emma Swallow lit up by moonlight holding my daddy in her arms. She rocked him like a little baby.

He pulled her face down to his and kissed her on the lips.

I ran back to my room.

I sat in my rocker by the window until light broke into the sky.

Next day I rode my bike. I tore up and down the asphalt streets of Cornwall Commons. I saw some kids playing. I knew them from school, but I rode right past. I put my head down low over the handlebars and didn't swerve for anything.

I came up the gravel driveway to my house flying and making that gravel explode away from my wheels. I skidded to a halt and dropped my bike.

Right there on the front porch, in front of the red gliders, I surprised my daddy kissing Emma Swallow on the mouth. When they heard me they jumped apart like two dogs from a hose.

"Issy," said the Prince.

"Isobel," said Emma Swallow.

So, they remember my name, I thought to my-self. I bent over the wheel of my bike and pulled Mickey Mantle out of the pocket of my shorts. I clipped him on a spoke of my bike with a wooden clothespin.

"We were just talking about the Cawdell Tent Revival," said the Prince.

"Yes," said Emma Swallow, "we were fixin' to take you there this evenin'."

We. Now it was we. We were fixin'.

"Yeah, well," said me. "I don't wanna go."

"You don't even know what it is," said the Prince.

"It's something stupid," I said. Mickey Mantle was just too bent up. The card had no spring left at all, he'd worn out. I searched in my pocket and replaced him with Ty Cobb.

"The Cawdell Revival is somethin', honey," Emma said. "It's a show and religion wrapped up in one. The first time I went I was around your age. I jist about couldn't believe it when your daddy told me he saw the sign posted out by the highway." She was leanin' over the porch railing, her eyes begging me.

"They had a sign every twenty feet or so. Big letters," said the Prince. "I guess they don't want to take any chances somebody might miss it."

"I thought you said churches weren't where you found God," I said to the Prince. "I thought you said God's in you."

"It's not really a church, Issy. It's kinda like a circus."

"Oh, it's not, Prince. It's not a circus at all. It's beautiful—all the singin' and, Isobel, people git healed! People who were lame can walk and blind can see. It's somethin'."

I looked up at them. They were leaning over the porch railing looking at me.

"I said I'd take you both," said the Prince. He looked out over my head.

"Please come," said Emma.

I wiped black grease off my hands on my shorts and stood up.

The Prince wouldn't look at me. I don't know what it was that Emma'd done to get him this way. He'd never go to church when Clematis used to take me.

"I'm busy," I said, looking at Emma Swallow.

The Prince looked down at me. "You're coming," he said. He walked in the house, letting the porch door slam after him.

Emma Swallow stood there looking at me with her silver-blue eyes.

There we stood. I stared her right down. "I know what you did with the fingernails," I said. "You put a spell on my dad."

"I didn't do that, Isobel."

"He doesn't love you."

Emma Swallow looked down at her hands, clean and tanned. "I know that."

I went up the porch stairs, sailed right past her. "My momma's gonna come back, she always does. She'll kill you. She'll take my daddy's gun from behind the bedroom door and shoot you clean between the eyes." I let the porch door slam after me, too.

I guess she just stood out there for awhile. I saw her at the porch railing through the window. She stared out to the road.

I expect she was looking for my momma.

But then, who wasn't?

seventeen

God in a tent

There must have been a thousand people all packed onto bleacher seats inside the tent. It was very hot and ladies and men waved paper fans to get some air going. I had one, too. It had a picture of Jesus with his hands held out and lambs kneeling down before him. There was a fat popsicle stick for a handle.

I was sandwiched between the Prince and Emma Swallow. People were talking this way and that, leaning over other folks' shoulders and shaking hands. A black lady down below me had on a hat with bumblebees on it. The hat was yellow and had black pipe-cleaners sticking up on it like candles on a birthday cake. The bumblebees were attached to the pipe-cleaners with threads. Every time she turned to talk to someone the bees buzzed around the top of her head as though her head were a hive with honey.

There were big spotlights and down on the stage was a small pulpit where the minister would preach. There were six or seven microphones lined up in front of the pulpit because the meeting was being broadcast on the radio all over the state. Behind the pulpit were more bleachers set up and two organs, one facing the other.

Everyone simmered down as the choir members, wearing gold and blue robes, started to file in and line themselves up on the bleachers.

The lights dimmed on our seats and bright spotlights set up high in the tent aimed down at the stage and lit it up bright.

The organs played together an opening run of chords that set people to leaning toward the stage.

"On a hill far away," sang the choir. There must have been two hundred of them down there singing "The Old Rugged Cross."

The people in the congregation started singing with the choir on the next song, "Go Tell it on the Mountain."

"Over the hills and far away," sang Emma Swallow, hitting a few notes and missing most.

The Prince just seemed to be watching the people. He looked at me and smiled.

I smiled back. I couldn't help it. Maybe Emma couldn't sing pretty, but she sure had the feel.

People started clapping and Emma Swallow took my two hands and clapped them together for me.

I clapped along.

The crowd was just about foaming at the mouth and me, I was starting to feel a glow running through me. Slowly and surely I got caught up in the excitement.

A man in a long, black robe came out on the stage. People clapped and rose up to their feet. Hundreds of voices came together and swelled up into the sound of a mighty storm.

"It's Reverend Cawdell hisself," said Emma Swallow to me. "Sometimes he sends his boy to preach. This bein' on the radio and all, I guess he wanted to make sure to come."

Reverend Cawdell lifted his arms up to the congregation. "My children," he said. "Stand in the presence of the one and only divine Lord God."

I looked him over. He wasn't God and I didn't see God standing anywhere near him so I kept my seat.

His voice boomed out to us, deep and rich.

"Let us pray," said the Reverend.

We all did the Shepherd's Prayer. Would goodness and mercy follow me all the days of my life?

"Tonight," said the Reverend, "we take our text from Galatians. When Paul was called to God he took his words into his breast. *His* words, brothers and sisters. He told the doubters that he was not a false prophet. Paul said, 'I did not receive the word from any man, nor was I taught it; rather, I received it by revelation from Jesus Christ.' Tonight we will all receive the word of Jesus Christ through our hearts. Tonight speaks the Lord our God. And I will speak to you from God, because, my lambs, because God has honored me." He hung his head down and covered his head with his hands.

"Ohhhh," sighed the crowd.

"Yes, I've been to sup at the Lord's table and my brothers, oh, my sisters!" Here he stopped and turned his face into the light. Tears ran down the sides of his nose. "I have brought with me this night his light, his joy!"

The organ began playing in the background "What a Friend We Have in Jesus."

"Tonight," boomed the Reverend Cawdell, "I want you all to give up your idea that Jesus is a being in Heaven. I want you to *believe* in your heart that Jesus is here among us and I promise you *he will be here!*"

"Amen," shouted people all around me. Emma Swallow was at the edge of her seat and her face had turned rosy pink. The Prince sat fanning himself.

I shouted "Amen!" too, but I was late. My amen hung out there in the air all alone, but nobody seemed to mind.

"Paul also told us, 'If someone is caught in sin, you who are spiritual should restore him gently. But be wary, or you also may be tempted. Carry each other's burdens and in this way you will fulfill the will of Christ.' "

I caught them in sin, I thought. I was tempted to smash Emma Swallow's nose, but when I looked at her, her crooked teeth hanging out in a big, gentle smile, I decided I would be as holy as Great Grandma Roundtree. So, I forgave her. I decided to work on becoming saintly.

"Let the light of the Lord wash over you. Let the light bathe you clean. The *light,* my friends, the *light* is the Holy Spirit, the Dove of God."

And I felt that light or something touching me. Might a been the heat in that tent, but then again it might have been an angel of the Lord. I was very determined to get washed clean.

There was more singing. As the night went on people took each other's arms and swayed like corn in a high wind.

"Come to me!" shouted Reverend Cawdell so loud his voice bounced off the top of the tent and rained down among us in echoes, booming like a thunderstorm. "Come to me that God may deliver ye of your persecutions!"

People who had been standing or sitting on the floor between the rows or bleachers began moving in a line toward the Reverend's raised hands. Helpers ran out into the line and helped people in wheelchairs or those who were blind. There were so many.

"I pray to Jesus, *heal* this man, that he may see thy light. *Heal.*" He banged the blind man on the head with his palm. *"Heal* him Lord Jesus."

We couldn't hear what the man said, but we saw him on his knees. The Reverend lifted him up and a woman led him away.

Into the microphone the Reverend said, "The fool says in his heart, 'There is no God.' I tell you they are *corrupt,* and their ways are vile." Reverend Cawdell hit another woman on an aluminum walker *bang* on the forehead. "*Heal* by the blessed power of the Lord!" And if she didn't push that walker over and walk in front of the crowd. Slow she went, each step a baby step, but she walked.

People around us started Hosannaing. Emma Swallow lifted her hands to heaven and moved her lips in prayer. The Prince pinched my arm and smiled at me.

"Having fun?" he asked me.

I was just about dizzy with excitement, the heat, the cleaning up of my spirit, and the miracles. I'd never seen anything like it.

My daddy patted my cheek.

Afterwards in the truck, Emma sat next to my daddy. I sat by the window. We laughed and giggled and stopped to get ice cream cones at Sobel's in Deer Lick. We didn't talk about the meeting, we all just felt it. We all felt washed clean.

Emma had on a new purple dress with little yellow stars on it. She smiled her crooked smile and rested her hand on my knee.

I watched the fields go drifting by, cows hanging their heads asleep, cleaned by the Holy Spirit. I figured animals must be included in the spirit washing.

The headlights picked up an animal crossing the road.

"Whew! Skunk," said Emma, and we all laughed and rolled up the windows till we passed by. Emma kept smiling that crooked smile.

We pulled down the driveway and saw, in the yellow glow of the kitchen window, a red school bus.

FABULOUS FAROHS it said in pale blue letters painted on the side. A black man was standing outside the kitchen door. When he saw us, he threw down his cigarette and said something to the kitchen door.

She came out the back door in an apple green dress. Her hair had been all cut off, and curls touched her forehead like kisses.

"Oh, Jesus," said the Prince.

Everything just blacked away, every minute that she'd been gone was dissolved into nothing and if I'd had to tell anyone right at that moment what was the story of my life, it would just have been her.

"Mommy!" I yelled and pushed away Emma's hand as I jumped for the truck door.

Emma kept smiling that crooked smile.

eighteen

Clematis Colton Roundtree

The Prince stayed by the truck looking at her from across the drive. I was moving toward her with dream feet, taking forever to get me where I was trying to go.

When I got where I was going I stood there and looked at her. She bent down, all smiles, and I jumped into her arms and almost knocked her over.

"My baby!" cried Clematis. "Here's my baby girl! Let's look at you. Lazy, look here, isn't she a pretty thing? This is my baby girl!"

I looked at the thin, black man who had been standing behind my mother.

"This is Lesley Jessup, honey. He's my main guitar man."

I looked down at his green patent leather shoes and up past the yellow pants and jacket to his soft yellow eyes.

"We all call him Lazy, though! Lazy Jessup has got himself a reputation, don't you, Lazy?"

"Yessir, little lady, I do got a reputation." He smiled at me. I hung onto my momma's hand, but I smiled back at him.

"Well, Prince, you just gonna stand there staring or what?" Clematis stuck her hip out and rested her hand there while she tapped her foot. "Lord, man, you look like you was seeing a ghost."

The Prince didn't move. Emma Swallow stayed

in the truck. I stood next to my momma, holding onto her hand. I could feel something in the air like heat lightning.

The man Momma called Lazy said something to her but she shook her head.

Emma Swallow opened the truck door and got out. The Prince stayed where he was, still staring.

Emma Swallow walked right up to Momma. Momma smiled. "Who's this, honey?" she asked me.

"Emma Swallow, Momma. She's our house-keeper."

"You got yourself a housekeeper. Now isn't that fine," said my momma. She looked Emma Swallow up and down.

"Pleased to know ya, I'm sure," said Emma Swallow.

"Pretty dress you got there," said my momma.

Emma hunched down her shoulders at my little momma. "I'll put some coffee on." Emma went in the kitchen.

"Tall thing, hum?" said my momma to me.

"Tallest woman criminal," I said.

"Criminal?" said momma. "We'll have to talk about that sometime. Can she cook?"

"She isn't really a criminal, she just can't go home. She cooks good." But Momma wasn't listening to me anymore. She'd started heading toward the truck, toward Prince.

He stood there looking straight at my momma, but not moving an inch.

I started after her, but Lazy Jessup grabbed my shoulder. He shook his head. "Let her go, child," he said.

I couldn't hear what she said. She reached out and touched the Prince soft on the chest. He looked at her, then reached out and touched her hair.

I heard her laugh. If I tell you her laughter was all

the sound of a bright summer day, could you hear it?

Next thing they were in each other's arms, kissing.

"Come on with me," said Lazy. "Let's get us some coffee."

"I don't drink coffee," I said as he steered me into the kitchen.

In the kitchen Emma Swallow had a pot perking and was setting out one of her berry pies with plates and napkins. She moved out chairs for me and Lazy, then started to leave the room.

"Where you going?" I asked her.

"Pack," said Emma.

"Pack? Pack what?"

"Sweet Jesus," said Lazy Jessup.

She left the kitchen, her head down. She was shrunken with sorrow. I hadn't thought at all. I hadn't thought about Emma.

"I tole Clemmie she shoulda called first." I looked back at Lazy Jessup and his face was sad like he'd swallowed up some of Emma's sorrow.

I followed Emma Swallow up the stairs to her room.

She walked over to the old dresser with the cracked mirror and started pulling things out. I'd never seen her things before. She took out an old rat-eared Bible—King James version, the cover partly torn away; three blouses, folded neat—a pale blue one and two white; a skirt the color of coffee with turquoise rickrack stitched on it; an ugly orange nightie; and some cotton underpants. Off the top of the dresser she took a pink plastic comb and brush set and a silver bangle bracelet—only jewelry I'd ever seen her wear.

I sat on the bed and watched while she folded everything over again. She looked around the room.

"What are you looking for?" I asked.

"A sack, somethin' to put this stuff in."

I looked around the little room.

Emma had found an old grey and blue hook rug down in the basement and it was set on the floor next to the scratched fourposter bed. On the wall she'd taped pictures from magazines. I recognized the picture of the pyramids from *Life* magazine. There was a picture of mountains, big hills, really, covered with trees. A stream wound down one of the hills. Another picture—this one in color—was a bunch of flowers, pink, red, yellow, and white. I think they were some kind of wildflowers in a chipped blue bowl. A black and white picture of a beagle dog with sad eyes was taped over the red and white vinyl chair from the kitchen.

One other thing.

She'd found my great grandma Roundtree's big black wood crucifix with the crying Jesus. She nailed that up above the head of the bed.

Emma took a plastic bag from the back of the closet. She put all her things in it and took her three other cotton dresses off the wire hangers in the closet. She put them in there, too—the swan dress, the one with red roses, and another checked thing with frayed cuffs that she wore during the day around the house.

"That about does it," said Emma.

I pulled the white fringed bedspread over my head.

"Stop that, Isobel," she said.

"I'm a ghost," I said under the spread.

She didn't answer me. I heard her doing something. I peeked out of an eyehole I made with my finger in the bedspread.

She poured the stuff out of her neck pouch into a little bowl she'd had sitting on her dresser.

"What're you doing?" I asked and pulled my

head out of the bedspread.

She didn't answer.

I stood up on the bed to see over her into the bowl.

I saw some dirt—looked like regular old dirt—a little bone, so little it must have been from a mouse or something, a bluejay feather, small one from the wing, a piece of yellow yarn, some white hair—could have been from a dog—and my dad's fingernail pieces. She lit a kitchen match and set a piece of Kleenex on fire and put it in the bowl.

It stunk bad and made grey smoke that rose up in front of the mirror.

"Why are you doing that, Emma?"

"Why not?" she said, and she was crying.

"Dirt don't burn," I told her.

She picked up the bowl, just stinking now, and dumped all the stuff right out the window.

"That's your witch stuff!" I said, hanging out the window. I saw where it landed behind the evergreens on the side of the house.

"I'm no witch. Can't tell fortunes worth a damn neither."

I'd never heard a bad word come out of Emma's mouth before.

"Sure you are, Emma," I said. "I've seen you dancing and stuff by the garden at night. You're a witch, but I think a good witch."

She sat down on the kitchen chair and leaned out the window.

"Emma, why you gonna leave us?"

"You don't need me now, Isobel. Your momma's home."

I walked over by her and sat right down on her lap. I wrapped my arms around her neck.

"I need you more'n ever, Emma Swallow," I said.

"Hush, now," she said. But she didn't cry.

She rocked me on her lap, back and forth, and me such a big girl. We held our arms tight around each other for awhile.

Pretty soon she stood up and set me down. She looked me in the face and I smiled up at her.

"Let's go downstairs," Emma said.

I snuck up to her room while she was serving coffee to Lazy, the Prince, and Clematis.

I took her things out of the plastic bag and put them away, nice and neat.

nineteen

Music

"We had us a rockin' time up to Chicago, didn't we Lazy?"

Clematis was drinking a rye and ginger ale.

The Prince, Lazy Jessup, Emma Swallow, and me were sitting with her out in the front room. The sun had just gone down and crickets were chirping outside the windows.

"We did, we did," said Lazy. Lazy was picking at a beat-up guitar that he had taken out of a black guitar case. The case had stickers on it from California, New York, Mississippi, and other places I'd never been to.

"Now I have to tell you," said Clematis and she winked at me, "I never had cooking like that dinner you made anywhere on the road."

Emma Swallow bent over in her chair and picked up a dustball off the rug. She rolled it back and forth between her fingers.

"Miss Swallow, I hear you're from down south aways," said Clematis.

"That's right," said Emma. She talked so soft it was hard to hear. She was looking at Clematis.

Clematis sat like a queen in the green armchair. She'd put on new lipstick after dinner—it was dark red. Her skin was pale next to it. She had on nail polish to match and a pretty ring with an aqua stone on her pinky finger. She fanned herself with the *National Geographic* she'd picked up off the coffee table. She fanned and sipped on her drink.

"It been this warm for long?" she asked nobody

in particular.

"It's been awful hot, Momma," I said. "I get all sticky at night and wake up all wet. One time I thought I'd wet the bed!"

Everybody laughed but Emma Swallow. She'd found a loose thread on her hem.

The Prince didn't say anything. He sat on the sofa next to Lazy Jessup and couldn't seem to wipe the smile off his face.

"Aren't you something," said my momma. "I can't get over how pretty you got in just ten months. Oh! Was it that long? You got my card, you got my letters?" she asked the Prince.

"I got three letters," he said. He stopped smiling.

"I got a card, Momma! It had a Lassie on it and that picture of you singing!"

"That's right," said my momma. "I meant to write more, to keep up and all, but we were so busy. Things was happening so fast, wasn't they, Lazy?"

"That's right," said Lazy as he picked out a crazy, wailing "Camptown Races."

"We got that booking up in Chicago. That's when we put together the Farohs—the name was Lazy's idea. He likes Egypt. He wants to paint pyramids on the bus!"

Lazy grinned and answered her back with a long whine on the guitar.

"Lazy here played with Albert King down in Mississippi. I am the lucky one! He heard me singing in a club in Gary and took me under his wing."

"You took me," said Lazy.

"He'd been working at a steel mill, stopped playing a few years back."

"My wife'd been sick," said Lazy as he played.

"He said I could wail, that's what you said," said my momma to Lazy. Lazy kept grinning and playing. I watched his fingers flying up and down the neck of the guitar.

"Can you play with your eyes closed?" I asked him.

He closed his eyes and played something fast and slick.

"We got together and started practicing some, put together a few numbers, then he got Golden Boy and Bouncin' Joe Jackson to come over to my motel in the evening and work out with us."

"How come you're named Lazy?" I asked him.

He looked at me, his eyes flashing in his head, big smile aimed right my way.

"Lazy's got a way with the ladies," laughed my momma. "Anyway, Bouncin' Joe'd bring over some hamburgers and we'd practice till two or three in the morning. Manager didn't like that one bit."

"Fattest man ever played the sax," said Lazy. "But he can wail some, I'll tell you that."

"Who?" I asked.

"Bouncin' Joe," said Lazy.

"Anyway, before you know it the Fabulous Farohs was formed and we were giggin'. It was what I needed to get heard serious. And you'll never guess what happened last!"

"What happened," I asked.

"Well, I've come to tell you. I mean I woulda come sooner and all, but this happened and it was like boom! Things started rolling. We left the rest of the band up to Chicago. There's six of us now. Here's the thing."

"What, Momma?" I asked.

The Prince sipped on his Pabst Blue Ribbon and looked out the window. It had started to rain.

"A man by the name of Sam Berstin was at the Holiday Inn one night ..."

"Bernstein, Clemmie," said Lazy.

"What?"

"The man's name is Bernstein, not Berstin."

"Bernstein. His name is Sam Bernstein. He wants to sign us!"

Everybody was quiet. I didn't know what she meant, but the Prince must have. I could tell by the set of his face.

The telephone rang. It was sitting on a side table right next to the Prince. "Hello?" he said. He kept his eyes on Momma's face.

"Well?" Clematis leaned out of her chair, staring at him. "Who is it, honey?"

"I changed my mind," said the Prince. "No, I don't care. No." He hung up the phone.

"Who?" asked Clematis.

"Potter," he said.

Wasn't I a know-it-all? "He wants daddy to sell the woods for lots of money!"

"Really? Honey, that's so perfect! Will he buy the rest, the whole place?"

He stared at her.

"Well?"

"Sign you how?" he asked.

Clematis's face lit up. She forgot her question. She put up her arms in the air like she was leading a symphony. "Well, sign us up to a record label, of course! And not just any record label. *The* record label—*RCA!*" Clematis's face was glowing pink. Her perfect teeth were showing in a big grin. "Don't you see! We're gonna get rich!"

"Can I get a horse?" I asked.

"Sure, honey," said my momma. "You can get yourself two horses and some pretty new dresses and we'll all move up to Chicago and live in one of those high-up apartments with a view of the lake."

"We like it here fine, Clemmie," said the Prince. "And you know it." He tossed back the last of his beer and crunched the can up with one hand.

"Honey, now you know this is just about the best thing that ever happened to me, 'cept for you of course, and when you sell this place, we'll be set!"

Clematis went over to the Prince and sat down on his lap.

Emma Swallow got up and started collecting the beer cans that the Prince and Lazy Jessup had left lying on the floor.

"Oh, honeybear," said Clematis to the Prince, "you'll like it fine up there." She rubbed her two hands on either side of his face. He sat there not moving. "Won't you look handsome in a dark blue suit?" Clematis leaned down and kissed him on the mouth.

The Prince stood up and dumped Clematis out of his lap. She thumped onto the floor.

"I gotta feed the hogs," he said.

He went out the front door into the rain.

Clematis got up from the floor and brushed out her green dress. "Pig," she screamed at him, leaning out the window. "You're the pig!"

Then she turned and smiled at me.

"What a pretty girl I got," she said.

twenty

They get acquainted

I went into the kitchen after Emma. I was right. She was sitting in there crying.

"What's wrong now?" I asked. "They always fight. It's just their way. Tomorrow they'll be kissing all creepy and stuff right here at the table. You should be glad," I told her, "that you never seen them really fight; then you gotta run 'cause my momma throws things and my daddy throws her."

Emma smiled at me, too sad.

"Here," I said, "I'm gonna braid your hair."

Emma had pretty brown hair with bits of gold that came out in the sun. She kept it back in a messy bun most of the time and never let it just flop around her face like mine. Sometimes after dinner I'd get a rubber band and while the Prince was out drinking with Elmo, I'd do it all in one long french braid real nice. Emma almost looked like a schoolgirl when I braided her hair like that.

From the front room I heard Lazy picking something awful sad and sweet.

Then I heard my momma sing.

My momma had sung to me since I lay in my cradle. Her voice would rock me right to sleep. I never heard my momma sing with a guitar. Her voice alone had always seemed like the whole song.

She was singing this sad song.

"They call it stormy Monday, but Tuesday's just as bad," sang my momma.

I pulled open the junk drawer and got out a

green rubber band. "You just sit there," I told Emma.

She did.

I took the bobby pins out of her hair and fluffed it out with my fingers. Her hair wasn't as long as mine, only came down to her wingbones, but it was thick and felt smooth. Near her, I smelled baking biscuits and ripe apples.

I combed her hair with my fingernails and divided it into three pieces.

"That's the *best* day I ever haad," sang my momma.

I wove Emma's hair, keeping my fingers tight to keep the hair from escaping. The rain was really coming down. It started splashing in the kitchen sink through the open window.

The music in the front room stopped. I heard the front door close.

"That's momma," I told the top of Emma's head.

"She's going out to the barn to daddy."

Emma sat straight and tall in her chair. "Don't worry, Emma. I'll always need you." She shivered a bit.

"Did I hurt you?" I asked her when I pulled the hair tight.

She shook her head. I finished and went round the front of her.

"Emma," I said, "you look real pretty."

She got up and started washing the dishes in the sink.

"Whew!" said my momma as she came whirling in the kitchen. She turned around twice on her toes like a ballet dancer. "This rain's just making everything stickier." She sat down at the table. "Honey," she said to me, "bring me that bottle of rye whiskey offa that counter there, that's a dollbaby—no, no ginger."

I brought her the bottle and a clean glass. I

guessed it was Lazy Jessup that had gone out the front door.

"Why, Miss Swallow, your hair like that takes years offa you!" said Momma.

"She's twenty-nine," I said. I was proud I knew something she didn't.

"Well, that hairstyle makes you look closer to your age then," said Momma and she poured herself another drink.

"Thanks," said Emma. She didn't turn around from the sink. She had white soapsuds up to her elbows.

"My momma's thirty-two!" I crowed to Emma.

"Isn't that funny, Miss Swallow, people always take me for twenty-six at the most. If I was you, I think I'd bleach out that hair. That might do it."

My momma put her feet up on a kitchen chair. She didn't have on any shoes and her red toenails showed up bright against her white skin. My momma was always proud of her pretty little feet.

"It's just wonderful of you to care for my family like you do. I can see my girl's taken to you. I never was one for housework. Oh, I know that's a sin around here, but some of us just have other talents." She tapped her long fingernails on the tabletop.

"Momma, will you show me your dresses?" I asked.

"Later, lambie, bring me some of that pie there. I got to talking out there and forgot to eat. It's Miss Swallow's homemade, isn't it?"

I took her a piece of raspberry pie. She pushed it around on the plate with her fork. "Like I said, if you bleach out your hair that'd do you a world of good. I'd be happy to help."

She smiled at me. I sat down across from her at the kitchen table.

"Remember that time, Issy, that we bleached

your hair and surprised your daddy?"

"Oh, yeah, he was madder'n a hornet," I said to Emma's back.

Momma laughed.

"See, Miss Swallow, I got a bottle of peroxide down at the drugstore because I was gonna bleach out my hair. But when I poured that stuff in the warm water and those fumes hit my nose, I said, no. The Lord has blessed me with this red hair and who am I to dispute that? I left the kitchen to get something, I don't remember what. Oh, yes, the phone was ringin'. It was Prince calling from the auction to say he got a fantastic price on the spring stock, remember, Issy?"

I didn't remember that part, but I nodded and smiled anyway.

"Wouldn't you know it, the minute my back was turned this one here," she pointed at me and wagged her finger, "she climbs up on a chair and dumps the top of her head right in that sink with the bleach. I don't know how she knew what it was for. I didn't tell her. You were what, Issy? Six, seven?"

"Eight, Momma," I said. "I heard you talking to the drugstore lady."

"Anyhow, I come back in the kitchen and see her long hair floating in the sink. It was a miracle she didn't get any in her eyes. Well, what was I gonna do? Have a kid with hair that was two-toned? I just dunked the rest of it in there, too. You were a cute little blonde there for a month or so, Issy."

I remembered that water stinging my scalp. Later on I had scabs all around the edge of my forehead and down by my ears. I ended up with two-toned hair anyway, but the reverse. When my own brown hair grew out on top a couple of inches or so, Momma had the barber cut it all off in a pixie cut. I hated it.

"Now they got better stuff to use. We could do it

tomorrow," said my momma.

She poured another drink.

Emma turned around and wiped her hands on a dishrag. "I don't hold with dyin' hair. I believe you take what you get." Emma took off the yellow dotted apron and hung it over the oven handle.

"Sit down a minute, Miss Swallow," said my momma. "Take a load off your feet. Here, have a drink. Or, don't you hold with liquor either?"

"I have a drink occasionally, mostly beer," mumbled Emma.

"Emma was gonna leave," I told Momma.

"Goodnight," said Emma as she made for the door, but Momma had her.

"Leave? My goodness, whatever for? Do come sit down, Miss Swallow. I'd truly like to get better acquainted. I'd like to thank you again for being so good to my family."

"T'wern't nothin'."

"How cute you sound. 'T'wern't'—Why, my grandpa used to talk like that. He was from the hills in West Virginia."

"She's from the hills," I said, stirring things up.

"If you don't come sit down with me, I'm afraid I'm just gonna have to come over there and drag you." My momma put her glass down on the table with a bang.

Emma Swallow stood in the doorway.

"Come tell us about your family," said my momma.

"Yeah," I said, "come on, Emma."

Emma Swallow came and pulled out a red vinyl chair and sat down.

"Bring her a glass, Issy."

"OK, Momma." I put a little Welch's jelly glass in front of Emma.

Momma got up and came over to Emma and

poured her some whiskey.

"A toast," said Momma. "Let's drink a toast to the pig in the barn."

"Elmo?" I asked.

"We know who, don't we, Miss Swallow?" and Clematis raised her glass up in the air toward Emma. "They go into heat in the spring and like to rut all summer, don't they?" Momma drank her toast and poured out another. "They get too big and fat in the fall and that's killing time."

Emma drank her whiskey down in one swallow.

"I'm right, aren't I, Miss Swallow?" My momma leaned into Emma and grabbed her hand. She patted it.

"Don't worry," she said. "I don't get jealous. Who'm I to get jealous. Christ, I left my husband. I left my own damn kid."

I stared at my momma. Pretty soon she'd start throwin' stuff. The kitchen was a particularly bad place when Clematis lost her temper.

"Do ya love him, Miss Swallow?" Momma poured another drink for Emma.

Emma drank it quick. She looked Momma in the eye. "Do *you?*"

Momma put her head down and rubbed her face with her hands.

"That's none of your business," she said. She lifted up her face to me, then to Emma. "Fact is, I do. But what the hell," she said. "Have another drink. Tell me all about your ol' Kintucky home."

Emma said, "There's nothin' to tell."

"Uh oh, I smell a rat," said Momma. "My little girl here ..." She rubbed my back. I laid my head down on the table. "Said somethin' about a criminal?" Momma laughed, but this time her laugh curled up my toes.

"I don't know—criminal around my daughter?"

Momma looked at Emma, who had slunk down in her chair.

"Vagrancy," said Emma. "I ain't no criminal."

"Hum, vagrant. What's the story here? Confession time. I'll show you mine if you show me yours." Clematis leaned forward. "Come on, you can talk to me. I don't bite, do I, Issy?" She patted my downed head. "I forgot though, you do." She laughed that way again. "What's the story?"

Emma Swallow downed another jelly glass of whiskey and poured one more. She looked my momma over, leaned back in her chair and crossed her arms.

My momma looked straight at her.

I sat there, my head down on my crossed arms on the table, moving my eyes first this way, then that, to see who was gonna give.

"I don't have to tell you nothin'," said Emma Swallow to her right arm.

"Well, there you go," said Momma. "I figured that was your attitude. Guess you're right. You don't." Momma jumped up cat-quick and leaned across the table. She grabbed Emma's arm, then she grabbed her wrist hard, forcing her to drop her drink and spill it. "Who do you think you are just walking into my home and making off with my husband and my child?"

Emma Swallow sat there. She stared my momma down with her silver-blue eyes.

"I'm God's mercy, woman. You better git that straight."

My momma let go of Emma's wrists and sat back down. It seemed all the air went out of her and she folded up and banged her forehead down on the table. Her shoulders were shaking and loud crying noises were coming from her bent head.

I put my arms around her bent shoulders and

laid my head down on her back. "You made my momma cry," I glared at Emma Swallow.

She just looked back at me.

"Don't cry, Momma," I told her shaking shoulders. "Don't cry."

My momma raised up her head. Her face was red and blotchy and there were wet spots on the front of her shiny green dress. She pulled me to her hard and hugged me. Her face on my neck was warm and wet. I started crying, too.

Emma Swallow tapped her fingers on the table. "I carried on with a man my daddy didn't like. He joined the service." Emma drank down her drink and pulled the bottle to her.

Momma and me looked over at Emma. Emma seemed to be talking to the refrigerator.

"He went AWOL one day and that was that," said Emma.

I brought Momma a napkin and she blew her nose. I sat down on her knee. Momma poured another whiskey and gulped it down. I bent my head into her chest and made myself into a little child.

"He just took off from the service?" asked my momma. "He just left you like that?"

Emma shrugged her shoulders and picked up her glass. She took her apron and wiped the glass dry and poured herself another drink.

I lifted up my head. I didn't understand why Emma couldn't go back home if the bad man was gone.

Emma slugged back her drink. Momma poured her another.

"Come on, honey, you can let it out." Momma looked at Emma with her head tipped to one side. She rubbed her cheek on mine then shook her head like she was trying to clear it out.

"I was pregnant. They don't hold with that

where I'm from, leastways not if a man don't step up and claim you."

"I have a feeling they don't hold with much," said Momma. "What happened?"

"I lost him after my man disappeared."

"Boy?"

Emma nodded. "I found him in the toilet one morning after I'd had some particular bad pains. I looked down to flush and there he was."

Momma looked at Emma and started to reach out her hand, but pulled it back. She held up the empty bottle and shook it. "Still keep the liquor under the sink?"

Emma nodded like her head was too heavy.

Momma moved me gentle onto the floor.

"Go on up to bed, sugarbaby," she said. "Emma and me are having a talk."

"I'll be quiet," I told her. "I'll be quiet as a mouse."

"Go on," she said.

But I kept sitting there and she got up to get her drink.

I couldn't believe it. Emma had found her baby boy in a toilet. That musta been awful, I thought. It must have fallen in there and drowned. That's why she had those sad dog eyes when I first saw her. Can there be a worse way to die?

Momma got a bottle of Wild Turkey out and planted it between Emma and her.

"Lord," said Momma, quiet. "Let me pour you a stiff one. Lord, honey. Your folks Baptist?"

"Pentecostal," said Emma.

"Lord have mercy," said Momma. "They do those thing with the snakes and all?"

Emma nodded again.

Momma was quiet a minute, her head swayed. "Lost one too, boy. Prince's boy." She saw me looking at her. "You would've had a brother."

And Emma had told me that, hadn't she? Read it off my palm. If I had had a brother and his name had been ... but Momma was patting Emma's hand.

"So go on, tell me what happened to that pig you married. He just run off when he knew you were expecting?"

Emma held her Wild Turkey between her fingers and rubbed it against her forehead.

"He died in a car crash."

"Good riddance," said Momma. She propped up her chin on her hands.

"I loved him," said Emma.

"Hell, honey, I loved the devil himself once, but good riddance."

They sat there quiet a few minutes.

Emma shoved her glass around on the checkered plastic tablecloth. It left rings.

"Hey," said Momma, "I'll tell you what. Issy, run into Mommy's room and dig in that blue overnight case and bring me the nail polish called Pure Sin."

I shoved off from the table.

"Run now," laughed Momma.

I looked and looked in the Prince's room for that blue bag and finally found it under the bed. Everything had spilled out of it. I put her stuff back and looked at all her makeup. She had Maybelline eyeliner and mascara. I put some on my eyelashes, but messed it up and smeared it. I had to get a Kleenex and wipe it off. I put on some of her red lipstick. Wildfire, it was called. My mouth looked like it had been sucking blood. I couldn't get it all off with the Kleenex so I wiped it with the back of my hand.

There were six or seven different nail colors and I had to turn them all over to see the names on the bottom. By the time I found Pure Sin I had been gone some time.

I went back to the kitchen with the polish and they were giggling about something. Momma put her finger over her lips when I walked in and they started giggling again.

Their eyes were shiny and the Wild Turkey bottle was almost empty.

"Shit," said Momma. "'Scuse my French, but I like you."

"Hell," laughed Emma, "we all got our problems." They started giggling again and this time Emma sent me up to bed.

Next morning Emma had deep red polish on her nails. A lot of it was outside the lines.

She wore it that way till it all peeled off.

twenty-one

Two weeks later

Boom! "Lyin' whore."

I heard them at it that night while I was laying in my bed. One thing I knew for sure—Momma was back.

This time things were different. We had storms for four nights in a row. It seemed some of that wildness got into the house and into our bodies.

In the front room Lazy's guitar took up half the couch when he got up and left it there—he often just wandered away, out the door. I'd see him walking along the electric fence toward town. Momma left clothes lying around when she got tired of wearing them, which was often. She changed her clothes at least four times a day.

"I get hot and sweaty," she said when I asked her why.

I'd tried on her high heels while she clapped her hands and Emma tried to look mad at me. She wrapped a soft purple rope of feathers around my neck one morning and let me wear it all day.

Emma was different. You'd have thought she and Momma had been best friends all their lives. Emma wore pink lipstick at the supper table.

After dinner Lazy would sing, then we'd all sing. I'd make up songs and Lazy would play along with me like I was a star. Everything would be going good and suddenly it would get quiet between songs and no one wanted to be the first to break the silence. Everyone would drift apart and the evening would die. We sang to keep the silence away, but it always found us around dusk. At twilight we became ghosts that just bumped into each other without seeing. We all knew something was bound to happen. The Prince was nice to Emma, but he treated her different, complimented her cooking a lot.

One night he said, "Miss Swallow, that was the best pork roast I've ever had."

Emma looked at Momma.

They both busted out laughing. I grinned, too, but I wasn't sure why.

"What's going on?" asked the Prince.

"Nothing, sweetie," said Momma. "Eat your carrots that *Miss* Swallow made."

"Hell," said the Prince and pulled his St. Louis Cardinals baseball cap down lower on his head.

He ate his carrots, then went out the back door. He stomped down the stairs real loud.

"You girls is bad," said Lazy Jessup. He shook his head all sad-like and went out to the back stoop and smoked a cigar. Then the silence came.

"You want it?" I heard the Prince yell at Momma that night.

Bang! I could hear it all the way up in my room.

Next morning they were at the breakfast table holding hands and looking into each other's eyes like something was lost there.

I think that even made Emma sick. She went up to her room till past lunch.

Later on, I saw my Momma sitting out next to the barn in the afternoon, sunning. She had on Hollywood sunglasses and a black one-piece swimsuit.

Emma was mixing dough for noodles. I watched while she sprinkled flour on the rolling pin and the kitchen table. She made a big ball out of the dough, then patted it with cool water from the refrigerator. Then she put a dish towel on the ball of dough.

"Can I help?" I asked. I wanted to go out in the sun with Momma, but I felt bad for Emma alone in the kitchen. The Prince had gone off somewhere in the truck and Lazy Jessup was right behind him in the red school bus. Lazy was getting the bus checked out at Snyder's Service Station. Lazy said the bus needed a new starter.

"I'm fine here, honey," said Emma.

I leaned down on my arms, then made a church out of my hands. Two thumbs for doors, two fingers for a steeple, the rest folded into prayer position.

"Look, Emma, here's the church, here's the steeple, open the doors and here's all the people!" I wiggled my people fingers at her.

Emma was rolling the dough out on the table and swatted me with the dish towel. "Move your elbows, Mabel," she said.

"Mabel, Mabel, get your elbows off the table!" I crowed while I flapped my chicken elbows at my side.

The rolling pin flattened down the dough ball. The dough then wrapped itself around the wooden rolling pin. Emma peeled it off and rubbed the pin with more flour. "Too sticky," said Emma. "I can't take this heat."

"Isn't it sticky where you lived, Emma?"

"Yep, sometimes. But mostly where my folks live at is cool because the house is built right up next to a sweet little river called Ghost Creek."

"Is it haunted?" I asked. I scraped some dough pieces off the edge of the table and rolled them into snakes. I coiled them so they could sit up, then used little pieces of dough for eyes so the snakes could see. I started lining little dough snakes around the edge of the table. Some I had sit up, others lay in squiggles. I started scraping the edges of the dough to make a big snake.

"Leave off with my dough, Isobel," said Emma. "Haunted? Why would it be haunted?"

"Ghost Creek, you said."

"Hum, spooks and such." Emma brushed back her hair out of her face. It had escaped from her usual messy bun on the back of her head.

"Well, I'll tell you, it might be at that."

I dropped my dough back on the table.

"What do you mean?" I asked.

"When I was little ..." said Emma.

"How little?"

"'Bout your age, I 'spect. I used to see something out my winda at night sometimes."

"What?" I leaned up against the table so I could look up at her face. "What?"

"Looked like a little girl in a pale-colored dress."

"What was she doing?"

"Fishin', it looked like." Emma wet a sharp knife over at the sink and started slicing the dough on the table. It was all flat now. The dough almost covered the table in one big sheet. She sliced with the knife, making long strips about as thick as my finger.

"Fishing? Why would a ghost be fishing?"

"Who said it was a ghost?" said Emma.

"You did," I said.

"I didn't," said Emma, "say it was a ghost, but fact is, I think it was. As to why it was fishin', why wouldn't it be? You think a ghost wouldn't like to fish?"

I shrugged my shoulders. "I thought they just liked to haunt things."

"Well, this little girl musta liked to fish. Fact is, there was a story that a little girl had fallen in the creek before I was born and drowned. That musta been her I saw out my winda, fishin'. As to hauntin', I think the dead sometimes get themselves stuck in time. Sometimes it's good, like that little girl—

happy—sometimes it ain't so good."

"You mean the ghost is sad?"

"I think so sometimes," said Emma.

I sat down on the kitchen chair and thought about that. Ghosts who were sad, happy.

"Can ghosts kill you?" I asked Emma.

"No," she said, "they can't. They got no power over the livin' at all. They's just pale things, honey. Like a picture in a magazine that got faded from time."

"How come I've heard stories about ghosts killin' people, then?"

"'Cause they's just scared. People are allus scared of things. Only way a ghost could kill you is if you let yourself get so scared that your heart gave out. Mostly you should pity them poor creatures."

"Did you ever see more ghosts?" Emma was sprinkling more flour on the noodles.

"There now," she said. "They's got to sit for a bit to firm up." She looked at me. "They's one that sits on the front porch in the evenin' and tries to catch lightin' bugs in his hand."

"There is?" My eyes were just about popping out of my head.

"He's very see-through, ain't much to him at all, kinda old gentleman. I git the feelin' he was full of fun. He's got hair that sticks out all around his head."

"Grandpa!" I said.

"Is it?" Emma wiped her hands on her apron. She was cool as ice water. She could see my grandpa's ghost and it didn't scare her one bit!

"Can I see him?"

"I don't know. If you haven't up to now, I doubt it."

"How come you can?"

She shrugged up her shoulders. "Don't know, Isobel. I always have from time to time. Different places, different people. I pretty much ignore 'em and they ignore me. Like I said, they's just kinda stuck somehow. I feel sorry for 'em and pray. Now don't tell nobody any of this."

"How come?" Emma was cleaning the flour up off the floor.

"People don't understand. I learned that a long, long time ago. It was bad enough bein' the tallest girl that ever walked on the face of the earth without havin' people know I could see spooks, too."

"But you did witchcraft and stuff," I pointed out.

"Not witchcraft! What I learned I learned from my granny. Mostly healin' plants. Cough medicines and the like. I learned a few spells. But when you throw spells you're askin' for trouble."

"What do you mean?"

"From Old Black Toes, the Dancin' Master."

"Who?"

"The devil man, child. Land, didn't you learn nothin' in your Sunday school?"

"Is that why you threw your witch stuff out?"

"Well," said Emma, "I was unhappy, see, and that stuff wasn't making me no happier, so I threw it out. I don't want no more help from Spirit Land. 'Sides, it gits dangerous and pretty soon you don't know which master you're servin'—the black angel or the white one. It's better to just serve the Lord."

I got a peach off the counter and stood there sucking and thinking. Emma kissed my forehead and set off for her room.

Emma had found the old *National Geographic*s that Grandpa Roundtree had kept. "I'm gonna read this whole set," she had told me a couple of days ago when she found them. "I'm gonna learn everything from Japan to Texas." I figured Emma was stuck some- where around Ethiopia where those women walked around with nothing on. I never got much past them.

I heard her door close to her room and pictured her up there, lying on her bed on her stomach. Naked ladies and men, painted red and blue, shook spears and danced with joyful faces while right on the next page, whales leaped out of the ocean like ships to the moon.

I looked out the kitchen window. Momma was turning a real pretty golden brown. I thought she was asleep under her sunglasses, but she waved me over.

When I got outside, she patted the blanket for me to sit down. I plunked down next to her. She had on Johnson's Baby Oil with iodine mixed in. In the bottle it was light pink.

"Want me to rub some on your back, Momma?"

"Sure, babydoll, let me take down my straps."

My momma pulled down the top straps to her suit, slipped them off her arms and lay her head down on her folded arms. I rubbed the oil on her, trying to get it even. I rubbed the leftover on my face.

"I'm already tan," I said.

"You look like a little brown Indian," she said. "Like Pocahontas."

I lay down next to my momma on the blanket. The sun cooked us together. A plane went overhead and zoomed over again. Momma waved and so did I.

"Crop-duster," she said.

We got lazy lying out there in the sun by the barn. I peeked with one eye and my momma's mouth was hanging partly open, so I fell asleep, too.

Next thing, I felt something different. I thought the sun had gone behind a cloud and I was pulling myself up from sleep to see. A dark shadow blocked the sun. I shaded my eyes with a hand and squinted.

The Cat Man had come for my momma and he stood between us and the sun.

twenty-two

A different love

"Wake up, Momma! Wake up!" I shook my momma by the shoulders.

"Hum," said my momma.

"Momma!"

"Whatsamatter? Stop it, Issy."

"Momma. The Cat Man."

My momma popped open her eyes. "Who?" She shaded her eyes like I did. She looked up at his face.

"Jesus," said Momma. She sat up on her elbows. "Johnnie?"

"Hello, darlin'," said the Cat Man. "I've been missin' you."

"Jesus," said Momma again.

"So glad to see you safe and sound, Clemmie." The Cat Man stayed above us, blocking the sun, blocking everything. I'd meant to tell my momma about him, but I kept thinking maybe he'd just been a dream, or now that I knew about Emma's spooks, maybe that's what he was—just a sad leftover of something that used to be real.

He was dirty, but it looked like he'd tried to clean up some. He smelled of strong soap—the kind you get out of the dispensers at gas stations. His red hair was fluffy and long and hung down to his collar in the back. His green eyes had bits of yellow floating around in them.

"Clemmie, Clemmie, Clemmie," said the Cat Man. "Clemmie Colton. How the hell are ya?" Johnnie Pearl sat down on the blanket at my momma's feet.

My momma sat completely still.

"This little piggy," said the Cat Man as he touched Momma's little toe, "went to market, this little piggy here," he said and grabbed her big toe, *"never* came home. Wee, wee, wee." The Cat Man smiled at Momma.

"Go in the house, Isobel," said Momma.

I looked at her.

"We know each other," said the Cat Man. "We know each other pretty well, don't we, Matilda?"

"My name's not Matilda," I said.

"Well," said the Cat Man, "you look like a Matilda to me." He smiled at my momma. "Here she is! I've met her already, Clemmie—you were hiding her from me all these years. Shame!"

"Run on, now," said Momma. She pushed me hard on the back. I got up and started toward the house. They were looking at each other so I snuck back quick around the barn behind them and scooted down behind a hay bale. I could peek around and see them while I lay there flat on the ground.

By the time I got hidden, he had pulled my momma like he'd pulled me to him—by the back of the neck.

He was going to kiss her. He didn't. He played around with her hair.

"You cut off your hair, darlin', that's a shame."

"Johnnie," said my momma, "when did you get out?"

"Why, sweetie, I been out for a long, long time. I've been hunting for you everywhere. I finally found you, though." He stroked my momma's hair.

"Everything's all right?" asked my momma. I couldn't see her face; her back was to me.

"All right! Honey, it's all wonderful. I get myself out of that loony bin and come huntin' for my dear sweet little wife and poof! She's gone. What do you think of that?"

"Johnny, you're hurting my neck."

"My love, I wanna do more than hurt your pretty neck. Clemmie, you're trash, sweetheart, pure trash. You know that, don't you?"

"Honestly, Johnnie, they said you'd be in there forever."

"Forever's a long time, ain't it?" The Cat Man let my momma go and looked over where I was. I ducked back behind the hay bale quick.

"The divorce was settled years ago. You know that. They sent you the papers."

"I never saw no papers."

"You did, Johnnie."

"I didn't sign nothin'," said the Cat Man.

"You didn't have to," said my momma. "The court ordered it final because ..." My momma looked down at her toes.

"Because I was locked up in the funny farm— incompetent? Right? Am I right?"

"Johnnie ..."

"So my wifey divorced me so she could screw everything on two legs and not feel a tiny speck of guilt." The Cat Man grabbed my momma again. This time he grabbed her waist, then pushed her down on her back. He lay there up above her. I could see the tops of their heads.

He patted my momma's face. "Poor little thing." He stood up.

The Cat Man pulled out a pack of Winstons and lit one up. My momma sat there on the blanket with her arms around herself. Wrapped up she was, like she was holding something in.

"So, my sweet little gal got herself remarried. Nice fella, ain't he?"

"He's nice, Johnnie. Good to me."

"Pretty little girl. What's her name?"

"Isobel. You didn't say anything to her?"

"After your long-sufferin' bitchy sister, right?"

Momma didn't say anything. She kept looking toward the driveway.

"Good thing she finally died of that cancer or I'd of been tempted to operate on her myself." The Cat Man smiled.

"Johnnie, you better get outta here. My husband'll be back soon."

"Get outta here!" The Cat Man snatched my momma's face with his hand and squeezed her right by her mouth. "Get outta here?" He hit her then, across the face. She fell on the blanket and held up her hands.

"You goddamned stupid bitch! I sit in a stinkin' hole for savin' your scrawny-ass life. I sit in there and sit in there forever, damn you, forever! I sit in there and to keep from goin' as crazy as the rest of those loony tunes, I think about what?" The Cat Man grabbed her again. "What?"

My momma didn't say anything.

"You! You red-haired bitch!"

"You shouldn't have killed him, Johnnie," said my momma to the blanket.

"That ratshit? That piece of shit who thought he'd slip around, putting his hands all over you. I shouldn't have killed him? I shoulda killed him better, slower." The Cat Man got up and walked around the blanket till he stood up at my momma's head. Now I could only see both their backs.

"I ain't unbalanced, Clematis, darlin'. It's you." He stood there smoking, looking down at her. "It's you. You know, don't you that you're the real nut, don't you?" He leaned over her shoulder and put his lit cigarette right next to her back. "Maybe," he said softer, "I shouldn't have ripped his nuts off, but it seemed just the touch at the time. I always was a poet, Clemmie. Wasn't I?"

He touched her back with the lit cigarette. She moved but just a little and didn't make a sound.

I felt dizzy there behind the hay. I wanted more than anything to run out there and help my momma, but I couldn't. I was stuck there behind the hay bale.

"Wasn't I a poet?" The Cat Man asked again. He moved the cigarette and bent down and kissed the spot he'd burned on her skin.

"You got a problem, woman. You got somethin' wrong with you that drives a man to death. D E A T H. You understand?"

Momma sat quiet.

"God, I loved you, Clemmie Colton!" The Cat Man hugged her from behind. I saw his shoulders shake and knew he was crying.

"Go on, Johnnie," said my momma in a quiet, calm voice. She never turned around.

He stood up behind her.

"You know, don't you, that you make me crazy?" he said.

Momma didn't move an inch. She sat like a statue.

"I'm goin' now, Clemmie, but I'll be back." He touched her curly head. "My love is like a red, red rose."

He walked off across the soybean field. I watched until he disappeared in the woods.

My momma sat there staring at the house a little bit longer, then she wrapped a towel around herself and went inside.

twenty-three

Visits and notes

I opened the door and Mr. Potter was standing on the porch. There was a skinny man with him dressed in blue jeans and a T-shirt. This man had an odor to him, something bad. He smelled like the Prince smelled after a day of butchering hogs.

"Daddy home?" Mr. Potter smiled at me. I hadn't been to Sunday school in ages—I doubted he remembered me.

"Isobel, right?"

"Yeah."

"Sweetie, you run and find your daddy. We got some business."

They came in the living room without an invitation. The skinny man ran his fingers over the furniture and looked all around the room. Mr. Potter parked himself in the armchair.

The Prince walked in and stopped short on seeing the visitors.

"Roundtree!" Mr. Potter's hands were out, reaching to my daddy.

"What's going on?" asked Daddy.

"I came to make you a final offer. I come to make it to you in person."

The Prince looked at the skinny man, who wouldn't look back at him. He leaned on the windowsill, looking out.

"I gave you my final answer."

"Why don't you sit and let's discuss this. Child, run and get me a glass of water. This is my associate,

Charles Sills. Chuck, sit down." I went nowhere. Chuck, the skinny man, went nowhere. The Prince kept standing.

Mr. Potter squirmed a bit in the armchair. His nice-guy smile was stretching his face out of shape. "Wellll ... you force my hand. Fifty thousand for the wooded acres."

"Get out," said Daddy.

"You're some bargainer—fifty-five."

"No bargains. I'm not selling."

"What'll it take, Roundtree, to get you to see how serious I am?"

"Goddamn you, I said no!" The Prince's face was red, his fists were clenched. Chuck, the skinny man, moved to stand behind Mr. Potter. He picked his teeth with a dollar bill.

"I worship the Lord, Roundtree. I don't profane him." He looked at me. "Especially in front of innocent children." He smiled at me. I went and stood by my daddy. I stood right next to him and I could feel him shaking. "You understand that I have got to get that land?"

"I don't understand nothing."

"Well, seventy-five thousand. Seventy-five thousand is a fortune. I hear that pretty wife of yours is back—likes pretty things as a pretty woman should and this one! She'll be a beauty and, as I recall, sharp, too. Money for college—in the bank!"

My daddy groaned soft. I don't think Mr. Potter heard him, but I did.

"I want you gone." My daddy was shaking like a leaf. I put my hand on his. "I want you and your goon out of my house and off my land."

"Goon! My Lord ..."

My daddy moved quick and opened the door.

They left. The skinny man's fingerprints were all

over everything. Even though I dusted he left a bad smell.

That same afternoon I found the first note. *Fireworks,* it said.

> *Come to the fireworks.*
> *Here in the trees*
> *on the greening moss*
> *with me.*

It was sitting on the porch rocker with a wilted daisy lying on top. I read it and put it back. A half hour later it was gone.

There were more notes for three days. I knew who they were from and I knew who read them.

twenty-four

She breaks hearts

I heard Momma and the Prince yelling in the bedroom, but I couldn't hear what they said. Emma, Lazy, and me were watching "Mr. Ed" on TV, but none of us were really paying much attention.

Earlier, Momma hadn't come in to dinner and I saw her out back talking to Lazy. Lazy was doing something under the hood of the bus. He looked like he was mad.

Around nine o'clock or so, Emma took me up to bed.

"Emma," I said, "what makes people bad?"

"I don't know," said Emma. "You wanna hear the goblin story?"

"Is it Old Black Toes?" I asked.

"Sometimes." Emma sat down on the edge of my bed. I'd put on my nightie. The wind had come up some and it was good to get some cool air in the window.

"Who do you think's bad?" asked Emma.

"I don't know," I said, "just people sometimes, I guess."

"Well," said Emma, "listen to this. Once there was a little..."

"The goblin story!" I said. And I lay down with the covers tucked tight around me.

"Once there was a little girl, who'd always laugh an' grin, an' make fun of everyone, an' all her blood and kin; and onct when there was company, an' ol' folks was there..."

I sprang right up in the bed and sang, "She mocked 'em and she shocked 'em an' she said she didn't care!"

"But—" said Emma, leaning down to me, all serious and stern, "*when* she kicked her heels to turn an' run an' hide, they was two great big ol' *black things* a-standin' by her side."

I yanked the covers over my head.

"An' then," said Emma, her voice deep and low, "they *snatched* her through the ceilin' fore she knowed what she's about, an'…"

I was already giggling.

"The *gobble-uns'll* git you if you *don't watch out*!" Emma tickled me considerable on the word *gobble-uns* and even harder on *watch out*. Then she stroked my back and hair until I calmed down and fell asleep.

The fresh wind through my window made me sleep deep even though I'd been sure I'd have bad dreams.

Next morning I heard slamming down in the kitchen. Pots flying, glass crashing on the floor. I ran downstairs because I didn't hear any voices.

I saw the Prince through the back window getting into his pickup truck.

The kitchen was a mess. The Prince had smashed everything. There was the cow's head that went to the cookie jar, but the jar was in a million pieces. The dishes looked like pieces to a puzzle and a chair had been thrown right out the window over the sink. I didn't see one place to put your foot down where it wouldn't get cut.

On the floor were pieces of paper. I stepped around the glass as best I could in my bare feet to get to them. I reached down and picked up the closest piece of paper.

… *in Chicago and I'll send you money,* it said. I

reached for another piece. ... *best this way ... I'm just not right ... not fair to ...* I found a pretty big piece. *I'm sorry you found out—I never meant to hurt you, you were never supposed to know. I love you always.* The rest of the paper was ripped to shreds.

I sat right down there on the glass-covered kitchen floor. I was so tired. I picked the glass out of my feet and watched the red spots well up.

Emma Swallow found me like that and kept me with her the rest of the day. I just wanted to sleep. I was so very tired.

The Prince didn't come home for dinner. The house was quiet with just the wind flapping the curtains at the windows, and when dark came, I crept into bed with Emma and she hugged me to her.

Later on I heard the chug, chugging of the Prince's pickup and the sound of his boots crunching on the gravel in the driveway.

Lying there in her arms, I smelled Emma's smell—warm ground and cherries is what she smelled like that night. Then I fell back to sleep.

I woke up choking. Emma lay next to me, still as a dead body. Black smoke was coming in under the closed bedroom door.

I watched it for awhile, rising up. It was black and thick—my head felt so heavy. But then I heard a crash and the Prince called my name. Then I knew. I shook Emma as hard as I could.

"Wake up," I said. "Emma, wake up. There's fire."

The Prince crashed through the door and grabbed me quick. He patted Emma's face, then slapped her hard.

"Daddy!" I screamed.

"Emma!" said my daddy, loud. She didn't wake up. "Help me wrap her in this blanket."

My daddy threw me the blanket off the bed.

"Why, Daddy?" I asked.

"Do it!" he yelled.

I heard something else fall with a crash and I was starting to choke from the smoke. Emma came awake and struggled. We'd wrapped her up like a mummy. "Lord!" screamed Emma. It came out all smothered by the quilt.

I thought I heard another voice calling from far away. My dad shoved me and Emma through the doorway.

We both stopped—Emma in her mummy quilt and me with a scream stuck to my face. The whole house was on fire downstairs.

Fire kissed and licked the banister to the staircase.

"Move!" shouted the Prince.

We moved. The Prince went first, then me, then Emma. A piece of the banister fell off at the bottom of the staircase. It looked like the whole front room was a sheet of fire. It was so hot I saw the walls start to cook, big bubbles like boils kept popping up and shrinking back into the wall. The smoke wasn't as bad on the staircase, but when we got to the bottom I started choking again. We stood there too stupid from the smoke and heat to move. Then a piece of the roof fell in with a crash. The Prince pulled on the front doorknob and screamed. It had turned white from the heat. I felt the hair on my head start to sizzle. The Prince kicked the front door and kicked it again. It collapsed, and flames jumped up from the little pieces of wood.

I heard that voice again, far away and calling out.

The Prince ran us off the porch. We stood out in front of the house, watching it burn. I saw something by the barn, I saw someone. The fire leaped up and I saw the shadow of a man. Then he ran into the woods and he was gone.

I never knew a house would burn like that. So nice and neat. First one part burned up, then another and another. The fire came out of the windows and stuck its tongue out at us standing there helpless.

My daddy sat down on the ground. He sat there like a lump and didn't say a word. Emma sat down next to him and put her arm around him.

I stood there and I saw another man, but this one was running toward the burning house. "Clemmie! Clemmie!" he sobbed. "Clemmie!" he howled.

I stood there watching as he ran straight through the hole where the front door used to be. The porch sagged and fell off after he ran into the house. He didn't know that she was gone. He didn't know.

I could still hear him screaming, but what he said, I couldn't tell.

Then the house fell in on itself and it was over.

My daddy looked up at me. His face was black from the smoke. "Who was that? Did I see someone?"

"No, Daddy," I said. "It wasn't nobody at all."

Emma Swallow looked at me. Slowly she smiled. "Good," she mouthed at me. "Very good." She hugged my daddy. He didn't move an inch.

I shivered in the hot summer night and was shivering still when the firemen came to spray hoses on the black smoke that was all that was left of our house.

They gave me doughnuts. I sat in the cab of the fire truck and ate them all—ate them until I was sick enough to throw up and did.

My dad walked in circles around nothing.

Emma Swallow talked to the fire chief.

There was a blank space where our house used to be.

I couldn't have stopped him—he ran into the

flames as though he were running into her arms. He didn't know that she was gone.

twenty-five

I ask Mr. Potter some religious questions

The police came and took my daddy away. The firemen had found a gas can behind the sycamore tree by the barn.

The policemen asked me questions. They asked Emma Swallow questions.

"Did your father wake you up from upstairs or downstairs?" The policeman was Sergeant Halloway of the State Police.

"Upstairs," I said to his little mustache.

"When did you first smell smoke?"

"When I woke up," I said.

Sergeant Halloway wrote something in a little green notebook.

"Did you see anyone the night of the fire?"

"Yes," I said. "I saw Emma."

"Anyone else? Anyone suspicious?"

"Chuck."

"Chuck who?"

"Mr. Potter's friend."

Then he wanted to know who Mr. Potter was. I told him.

Emma was sitting on the pull-out couch in the trailer. I was sitting on the pull-down bed. Another policeman was asking her questions. I heard her say, "I saw somebody, quick like, couldn't tell who. A man, certain it was a man," said Emma Swallow.

They brought the Prince home after finding out

he didn't have any insurance anyway. Didn't make sense to set fire to your own house for nothing. They sent out a team of policemen who wore gloves and sifted through the ashes. They found bones. When they questioned Mr. Potter he said he never heard of anyone named Chuck. Said I was a confused child.

The Prince wouldn't talk at all. At first he cried quietly. Then he stopped crying and stopped doing everything except feed the hogs.

I tried to open one of the windows in the trailer. You had to turn this little handle to get the skinny window to open. It was stuck.

The blue and white trailer said POTTER'S CONSTRUCTION in black letters on the side. Mr. Potter had lent us his workmen's trailer since we didn't have any place else to live. Mr. Potter had also offered money. He came out the day after the fire with his little girl, Sally.

"We are so sorry," Mr. Potter said to my daddy, "to hear about your loss. The Lord sometimes works in mysterious ways. I'm certain that out of this devastation some good will come."

My daddy didn't even look at Mr. Potter. He didn't pay him any attention. He just sat on his lawn chair with his rifle over his knees.

Emma and me had slept a bit in the cab of the pickup. Daddy didn't sleep. He just took his gun off the rack and parked himself in a lawn chair.

Mr. Potter looked nervous. His little girl Sally was younger than me—six or so. She had a face that made me think of a poodle dog—big eyes, long snout, and silly curled-up hair. She pranced around her daddy and peeked from behind his legs at me like she was going to snap at my ankles.

"That's so kind, I'm shore," said Emma.

"By the by," said Mr. Potter, looking at me, "we

haven't seen little Isobel in Sunday school for quite some time."

"I don't believe in God," I told him.

"Isobel!" said Emma.

"Well," I said to her, "I don't. Not his God anyway. Doesn't make any sense. Nobody could live inside a whale."

"Those are parables, child," said Mr. Potter. "You are supposed to see the meaning of God's love in the stories."

I looked at Sally who was squirming around, flapping up her dress to show off her pink underpants behind her daddy.

"Then how come God makes some people go to hell? If he forgives all sins then he should let everyone into heaven."

Emma looked at me. Her mouth didn't smile, but I saw that silver twinkling in her eyes.

"That's why you need to come to Sunday school. We explain these things. But actually, this is not a time for theosophical discussion. Mr. Roundtree doesn't seem communicative. I understand, I understand. What a loss." Mr. Potter glimpsed Sally out of the corner of his eye lifting up her dress.

"Stop that, Sally." He smiled at us and brushed back his too-black hair off his forehead.

"I asked you about that last year and you told me to sit down and not talk for the rest of the morning." I glared at Mr. Potter.

"About what?"

"People going to hell!"

"Hum," said Mr. Potter, "I don't recollect. I'm sure there was a reason." Mr. Potter looked at the Prince sitting in his lawn chair. My daddy had been watching, but as soon as Mr. Potter looked over he turned his head away.

Mr. Potter leaned into Emma. "I understand that

wife of his ran off again. That kind of woman is not good for any man."

Mr. Potter quickly moved away from the look in Emma's silver eyes. He collected himself. "I may have forgotten to mention," said Mr. Potter, "that I'm still very interested in purchasing this land here. I hope," he coughed a minute like there was a bug in his throat, "that I might help out by making an offer now."

"Well," said Emma.

The Prince took his gun and aimed it at a tree. He pretended to fire it and jumped back like it had kicked him in the shoulder.

"OK," said Mr. Potter, "let's set you folks up then." Mr. Potter had his crew boys tow the trailer up our drive and set it next to the barn.

"Just temporary, of course, I know," said Mr. Potter.

"'Course and our thanks," said Emma.

"I don't wanna live in a trailer," I said to Emma.

Mr. Potter's mouth jumped and twisted like it was doing a dance. I think he was trying to smile.

"You're poor people," said poodle Sally.

"You're a little creep," I said to her.

"Quiet, honey," said Mr. Potter to Sally.

Daddy kept sitting in his chair. He didn't even look over when they lowered that ugly tin-can trailer next to the hog pen. The hogs squealed. They didn't like it either.

"My daddy says you're poor people. We gotta help you," Sally danced around her daddy's legs. "We're Christians with charity!"

I reached out, grabbed her skinny little arm, and slapped her silly.

She screamed.

Emma grabbed me.

Mr. Potter's smile fell off and he just said, "Well ..."

"Thanks," said Emma to Mr. Potter. "Kids ..." Sally and her daddy turned tail and practically ran to their fancy blue car.

"Look here, Prince, we got us a trailer." Emma put her hand on his shoulder. My daddy cracked open his shotgun and put in some shells.

Now Emma and me were sitting at the pull-out table drinking some instant ice tea.

The police finally told Emma, while I was sitting on the black steps to the trailer, that the fire must have been started by a tramp, a vagrant. It must have been an accident or he wouldn't have burned himself to death. Maybe he'd been sleeping in the basement.

They closed the case.

"They didn't have nothin' to go on," said Emma to me that evening.

We looked at each other, then got busy—her peeling potatoes, me staring out the tiny windows at the bats that still swooped for bugs in the twilight air.

twenty-six

The tooth

We were still living in the trailer. I was supposed to start sixth grade, but I didn't go the first day, and I didn't go the second, and Emma didn't say anything and the Prince wasn't talking, so I decided to skip sixth grade period.

It was the end of September. The air was still warm during the day, but at night it was starting to turn kind of cool. We didn't have any heat in the trailer. We had blankets that had been given to us by people that felt sorry for us.

I saw Richie Levy one morning waiting by the bus stop. I walked over to him, but he pretended he didn't see me.

"Hey retardo!" I said.

He turned half around.

"Cootie boy!" I said.

He turned and looked at me and his face went all red.

"Yeah," he said. "Hi."

"You stuck-up or what?" I asked.

"I'm not supposed to talk to you."

"Why, 'cause our house burned down?" I decided to pretend like I'd never talked to his mom, like I didn't know anything about it.

"Nah," said Richie.

"Why then?"

"'Cause."

I picked up a good-size stick and twirled it at his face.

"How come, cootie boy?" I touched his chest with the stick.

Richie started twitching around in his shorts.

"'Cause your dad isn't married," said Richie.

I poked him hard in the chest with the stick. It went thrump. He backed up.

"Liar. He is too married."

"I don't mean to your mom, to that other lady, the tall one."

"Why should he be, retardo? She's our house-keeper."

"But you ain't got no house!" said Richie. He stood his ground and didn't back up any more. "My mom says she's not nice and that your mom is a whore."

Everything turned orange. I hit him over the head with the stick. When I looked down there was blood coming from Richie Levy's brown curly head. I shook his shoulder, but he didn't move. "Richie!" I said. "Richie!"

Mrs. Levy opened the kitchen door wide when I told her that her son was bleeding out by our mail-box. She pushed me out of the way and ran to get her Richie. She ran so fast her sunglasses fell off. I started to pick them up but left them lying there.

The rest of the morning I kept thinking that Mrs. Levy would come and bang on our trailer door. The Prince was out in the barn and Emma was sifting through the ashes from the fire.

She did that a lot. She found stuff. She found me a picture book only half burned up that I had when I was tiny. It was called *Legends Every Child Should Know.* The pictures had gotten black from the smoke. Emma also found melted money and my momma's ruby ring. The ring had melted only partly but the ruby was still pink-red in the light after I wiped it off. Emma gave it to me to keep. She found my stuffed rabbit, but he was scorched and he smelled like fire. I kept him on the pull-out bed I shared with Emma and she didn't make me throw him out.

One time she found a tooth.

She held it up to me. I looked at it. I went over and took it out of her hand. A pearly white tooth. A back tooth. I made a bag for it out of a scrap of cotton. I wore the bag around my neck on a string.

Mrs. Levy never came over to send me to jail.

For supper, Emma tried to make things to tempt the Prince to eat. Emma cooked in old pots and pans that the church group donated to us. We got food the same way. That night, Emma was working on a tuna noodle casserole. It was hard because the trailer didn't have an oven. Emma had to do it all on top of the two burners on the stove.

"Peel these here carrots, Isobel."

I did. "Emma," I said, "I did something today that I think I'm gonna get a pounding for."

"What's that, dumplin'? Do these onions, too." She handed me a bunch of onions.

"I swatted Richie Levy on the head."

"What for?" asked Emma.

"He said nasty things about you and my momma. So I pounded him." I looked down at the onions. "He was bleeding. I left him there in the road."

"My Lord! Isobel!"

"I told his mother," I said.

She pulled off her apron. "Come on," she said.

"Where?"

She grabbed my hand.

Standing at the front door of Richie's house I felt like I was gonna throw up. Emma knocked on the door three times but no one answered it. The lights were on. We could hear the TV going, but nobody came to the door. Emma pulled me by the hand around to the back. I saw someone look from behind a curtain by the sliding glass door, then they ducked out of sight. I think it was Rachel. Emma knocked on the back door. No one answered.

We stood back a bit and looked at the house. Emma looked down at me. I thought I heard a noise and looked up.

"Hey!" I heard a whisper. "Hey, Isobel, up here."

I looked and saw Richie's head sticking out his window. He had a big bandage around his head and under his chin.

"Richie," I said.

"Isobel, I'm sorry," hissed Richie.

I stood there with my mouth hanging open. *He* was sorry!

Emma nudged me with her elbow.

"I'm sorry, too, Richie. Is it bad?"

"Nah," said Richie. "I only had to have six stitches."

"Stitches!" I was stunned. I never got to have any stitches.

"Yeah. I didn't cry or nothin'," said Richie. "I think it's gonna leave a real cool scar."

"Really?" I said.

"Hey, Isobel," said Richie, "want me to come over and show you my stitches tomorrow?"

"Hey, yeah," I said.

Then Richie got snatched back through the window. His head disappeared. I saw his mom pull the drapes shut, but not before she stared down at where we were standing.

"Bye, Richie," I whispered. Emma gave me a kiss on the top of my head. We held hands walking back to the trailer.

"You did the right thing—he's a good boy, I think."

A firecracker went off. We jumped. But then we

knew it wasn't a firecracker. Emma looked at me.

Then I knew what it was. It was my daddy's double-barrel shotgun and the shot came from the barn. Emma knew it just as soon as I did. She screamed and tore off running for the barn.

I was right behind her. We got to the barn door, but we couldn't open it. The wooden latch had been dropped from the inside. Emma screamed again and tore at the door with her fingernails. "Prince," she screamed. "Prince!"

I ran around to the sycamore tree and climbed it like a monkey. I got through the window and into the hayloft, then climbed down the ladder to the floor of the barn.

Outside I kept hearing Emma's fingernails tearing at the door. She was howling like a dog.

The first thing I saw on the straw was blood, lots of blood. The hogs in their pens were grunting and moving nervously. They smelled the blood, too.

I got Jello legs then. I didn't think I could look around the corner and see what the blood was coming from.

"Prince!" screamed Emma Swallow in that dog voice.

I closed my eyes and moved around the corner.

I saw my daddy, his legs out in front, leaning back on a big tire of the little lawn tractor. His shotgun was laying over his knees. In front of my daddy lay Elmo. Elmo's ears, eyes, and snout were gone. On the floor was blood and I guess the grey stuff was Elmo's brains.

"Daddy?" I said.

The Prince looked at me. He looked like he had never seen me before. Great big tears hung in the rims of his eyes but didn't fall out. He looked away.

"Issy," said my daddy. "Issy, I'm a coward."

He put his head down and moved his hand back

and forth over his shotgun, like he was soothing it, calming it down.

It hit me then that my daddy was going to shoot himself after he shot his best-loved hog. I looked at my daddy and the thought of the less fortunates jumped into my head. I determined right then that I wasn't going to be one. I saw the Prince leaning on the lawn tractor. I could see the words JOHN DEERE printed on its green sides and for a moment I thought of my great grandma riding out of the barn, naked, big, and whooping her war whoops. I ran to my daddy then. I didn't even care that Elmo looked worse than any horror movie and that I was getting blood and guts all over my shoes. I ran to my daddy and threw myself in his arms. I kicked that shotgun away. I laid my hands on my daddy, on his face, on his chest and arms. I gave my all to heal him.

"Isobel!" screamed Emma. "Let me in!"

I held my daddy like I'd seen Emma do. I rocked my daddy back and forth and hushed his crying. I sang him a song I just made up. I don't remember it now—just sweet words and soft sounds.

Emma kept screaming, so I finally let her in.

Together we put my daddy to bed in the blue and white trailer.

I turned on the little portable black and white TV and my daddy stared at it until "The Star-Spangled Banner" came on and there was nothing left but fuzz.

My daddy lay down then, his arm falling out of the bed. He lay there and closed his eyes.

I climbed on top of him in the pull-out bed. I slept till morning light on top of his chest so I could feel him breathe.

"Shussh," went his breath in my ear. *"Shussh."*

I heard my momma singing in my head that night like she used to do when I was little and couldn't sleep and I felt filled up with her love.

twenty-seven

Where palm trees are

A letter came for me. The letter was in a large manila envelope.

The letter was from my momma.

"My darling baby girl," it said, "I hope this letter finds you happy. I guess sixth grade is pretty exciting. I have put fifty dollars in this envelope ..."

I looked down in the envelope and pulled out a fifty dollar bill. I smelled it. It was new. I set it out all smooth and nice on top of the pull-down table. There was something else in the envelope—a picture.

Clematis Colton it said in white letters in the corner. *Lyte Flyte Booking.* There was a phone number and then, *Los Angeles, California.*

Momma was in California.

In the picture my momma was dressed in a long black gown. Her shoulders and neck were bare and around her neck was a string of pearls. She had on long black gloves. Both her arms were stretched out, the way Jesus does in pictures when he's blessing people. She was smiling with her red lips and her eyes were smiling, too.

She was smiling at me.

There was a rose in her hair.

I taped her picture to the fake wood wall over the TV.

"... so you can buy some pretty school dresses. I have a job singing at a beautiful nightclub here in Hollywood. *Nothing* like anything back there. This is a class place and just last week Desi Arnaz was in and he sang a song with me! I even have my own dressing room and it's got a silver star on it. Issy, you would just love it here. The people are all so pretty and the sun, well, the sun shines all the time. Have you ever seen a palm tree? Of course not! There are palm trees growing right outside my apartment window. My apartment faces onto a swimming pool! My record contract is supposed to be ready for me to sign by the end of next month. They have to do some negotiating. Business, honey. Well, I better go. I have to go swim! That's how I keep my figure. I hope that Emma is taking good care of you and your dad. I know she is. I love you always, baby girl. Never ever let anyone tell you different.

"Love, Clematis.

"P.S. If you want to come out here in the winter, write me at the address on top of this letter and I will send you money for the bus or train. Maybe by then I'll be rich from my first record and you can fly on an airplane! Love again, Clematis."

When Emma came back in the truck I showed her the picture. She read the letter and I gave her the fifty dollar bill.

My daddy just lay in the pull-out bed and didn't notice that I'd taped Momma's picture to the wall.

"Keep it, sugar," Emma told me and gave me back the fifty dollars.

"But we should get a doctor for Daddy, Emma. He hasn't said a word or moved from that bed for two whole days."

"A doctor ain't gonna move your daddy." Emma started unpacking the bag she used to collect dented canned goods at the Kroger grocery store.

"You like sweet peas?" Emma held up a can.

"I hate peas," I said. I went over to my daddy. His eyes were open, but he wasn't seeing anything. Emma came and sat on the bed next to me and daddy.

"What's wrong with him, Emma?"

"He ain't got no heart left in him." Emma lifted his head gentle and fluffed his pillow. "It's all wrung out of him, honey."

"Will he get better?" I asked. I patted his hand.

"If we believe he will, he will. Believing in something really hard can make miracles happen."

"Do you?"

"I do," said Emma Swallow and she emptied a can of Campbell's Tomato Soup into a saucepan. When it was just lukewarm she spoon fed my daddy like a baby, keeping a napkin just below his mouth because he'd only swallow if he was about to choke. Most of the soup tended to end up on his shirt.

I turned on the TV and the Road Runner was on. My daddy and me used to bust up laughing at that Road Runner. I turned the sound up loud, but Daddy didn't even turn his head. I put my head down on his chest every once in awhile to check his heart.

"My momma doesn't know about the fire," I told Emma while she folded the clothes she'd washed out in a tub with the handpump.

"No," said Emma.

"I don't want to tell her," I said.

"Why not?" asked Emma.

"It's better that way," I said. I patted Daddy's hand again. He'd closed his eyes.

"She'd only worry and feel real bad," I said. "Emma, are we less fortunate?"

"What do you mean by that, Issy?"

"Less fortunate, you know, the less fortunates." I picked up my rabbit that smelled like fire. I buried my head in it for a minute or so. "Beep, Beep," said the Road Runner. Wile E. Coyote had just been mashed to a pulp with an Acme hundred pound weight. By a miracle, he pumped himself back into shape.

"I'm not less fortunate," I told Emma.

"Good. Come help me fold these socks and things."

I helped Emma fold. I folded each pair of my daddy's boxer shorts into four squares and pressed down on them to make them flat. I made a pile of them and started in on matching the socks.

On the TV Tweetie Pie was telling the old lady, "I tawt I taw a puddy tat." I glanced over at my dad, but his eyes were still shut.

"Did you know," I told Emma, "that when my daddy was small he almost died of snakebite?"

"That so?" said Emma smiling. "How'd that come about?"

"Well, see, he was only about seven or eight and he was walking out by the back woods."

I stopped for a second. I looked over at my daddy. "He crossed over a stump of rotted wood, and curled up there, pretty as you please, was a big 'ol rattlesnake as big as my arm, well my daddy, he just about ..."

"Copperhead," said a stranger's deep voice.

Emma sucked in her breath.

I turned to the pull-out bed. "What, Daddy?"

"Copperhead, there aren't any rattlers in this state."

"Copperhead," I said soft to Emma while I watched my daddy try to sit up. I talked louder. "This snake was as big as my arm and it was out there sunning and my daddy tripped over it and it bit him."

My daddy stared at me for a minute like he wasn't sure he knew who I was.

"What?" said the Prince, my daddy.

"Copperhead," I whispered to him.

"Snake musta been at least five feet long," said my daddy, sitting up now and kinda swaying a bit on the bed. "Well, that snake lit into my leg ... say,

Emma, where's my smokes?"

"They're right here in your work shirt where you left 'em." Emma handed my daddy a pack of Camels.

He lit one up.

He looked around our little trailer and saw my momma's picture on the wall.

We were frozen, Emma and me, staring at my daddy, the underthings half folded on the table. We watched my daddy look at Clematis, my momma.

"Sssssufferin' ssssuccotash!" said Sylvester, the cat.

Momma smiled out at him. She smiled out at us.

He sucked up some cigarette smoke.

"Ever seen a copperhead, Issy?"

I shook my head, no.

"Well," said my daddy, "their skin glows a dull gold ..."

I sat down on the bed next to my daddy, a pile of his unmatched socks in my lap.

"You got 'em down by Ghost Creek, Emma?" asked my daddy. He looked at his cigarette. "Whew, these boys are strong."

Emma nodded. "We got 'em."

"I used to go hunting for tadpoles in the spring and that's how I ran into this fella ..."

I leaned up against my daddy's shoulder. I could see my momma holding her arms out to us above the TV.

I loved it when Emma smiled that picket fence grin. I loved it when the Prince, my daddy, smiled back.

twenty-eight

I think Emma knew

The Prince doesn't know that I know, but he's my daddy. Always will be.

I went back to school. They made me, the two of them. They've started acting like parents all of a sudden. Clematis signed her record deal. We'll see what happens, but she's sending money every month. Prince started working on plans for a new house. It's going to have sliding glass doors, but no garbage disposal. "What do you think we have hogs for?" says Daddy.

All I have is the tooth and a letter he left her. I took one off the porch and kept it. Maybe that was wrong because my momma never saw it, but I figure she already knew all about him and it's my only way clear through to his heart. It was a poem.

> *I can't stop tumbling*
> *over and over in my*
> *mind that wildfire*
> *hair and that beating heart*
> *and rose and rose*
> *I hold you near*
> *is it sharp?*
> *the memory*
> *cuts*
> *if my hands are cold*
> *it's because I'm frozen*
> *wild and wasted*
> *and the wilderness*

is cold
bring me fire
bring me heartache
bring me distance
kiss matilda
child of backseats
and blues strung nights and deep dark al-
leys
and the smell of
your hair
heaven help me
or no one will.

My father wrote that. My father's dead and he died of love. I think in a way that's like a miracle. I wrote my mother and told her, told her everything except about the tooth and poem. I keep them always next to my skin. These are my witch things now.

I am part Indian, part runaway dreamer, part Cat Man. My great grandmother was a healer. She healed by hand.

This is my life story. Up to now. It isn't always pretty. But I keep climbing toward the light because I just can't help it and, I believe it's there.